THE LIGHT AT THE END
OF THE ROAD

Ginny Baird

THE LIGHT AT THE END OF THE ROAD

Published by
Winter Wedding Press

Edited by Martha Trachtenberg
Proofread by Sally Knapp
Cover by Dar Albert

About the Author

From the time she could talk, romance author Ginny Baird was making up stories, much to the delight—and consternation—of her family and friends. By grade school, she'd turned that inclination into a talent, whereby her teacher allowed her to write and produce plays rather than write boring book reports. Ginny continued writing throughout college, where she contributed articles to her literary campus weekly, then later pursued a career managing international projects with the U.S. State Department.

Ginny has held an assortment of jobs, including schoolteacher, freelance fashion model, and greeting card writer, and has published more than twenty works of fiction and optioned ten screenplays. She has also published short stories, nonfiction, and poetry, and admits to being a true romantic at heart.

Ginny is a *New York Times* and *USA Today* Bestselling Author of several books, including novellas in her Holiday Brides Series. She's a member of Romance Writers of America (RWA), the RWA Published Authors Network (PAN), and Virginia Romance Writers (VRW).

When she's not writing, Ginny enjoys cooking, biking, and spending time with her family in Tidewater, Virginia. She loves hearing from her readers and welcomes visitors to her website at http://www.ginnybairdromance.com.

Books by Ginny Baird

Holiday Brides Series
The Christmas Catch
The Holiday Bride
Mistletoe in Maine
Beach Blanket Santa
Baby, Be Mine

Summer Grooms Series
Must-Have Husband
My Lucky Groom
The Wedding Wish
The Getaway Groom

Romantic Ghost Stories
The Ghost Next Door (A Love Story)
The Light at the End of the Road
The House at Homecoming Cove

Romantic Comedy
Real Romance
The Sometime Bride
Santa Fe Fortune
How to Marry a Matador
Counterfeit Cowboy
The Calendar Brides
My Best Friend's Bride

Bundles
The Holiday Brides Collection (Books 1–4)
A Summer Grooms Selection (Books 1–3)
Real Romance and The Sometime Bride (Gemini Edition)
Santa Fe Fortune and How to Marry a Matador (Gemini Edition)
Wedding Bells Bundle

Short Stories
The Right Medicine (Short Story and Novel Sampler)
Special Delivery (A Valentine's Short Story)

Ginny Baird's

THE LIGHT AT THE END
OF THE ROAD

Chapter One

Samantha Williams centered her hands on the steering wheel and peered through the windshield. Fog crept up the glass as ice streaked it from the outside. The windshield wipers whipped back and forth, battling the frigid onslaught. Sam reached out a hand to adjust the windshield defroster, cranking it up a notch until it gusted full blast. Inch by inch, the dark road became visible beneath an arc of clearing fog, headlights haunting the eerie path before her. She hadn't seen another car in more than forty miles.

This wasn't the route Sam normally took at night. She certainly wouldn't have selected it on purpose, given the dangerous weather. Sam rarely took back roads home anymore. But a tractor-trailer had jackknifed along a steep incline on Highway 64, tumbling sideways and dislodging barrels of hazardous chemicals. One of the officers from the highway barricade had told her about it, recommending she take a detour. He suggested even more strongly that she get off the road. This early spring ice storm had caught everyone by surprise, including the Virginia Highway Patrol, he'd said with a polite smile and a tip of his hat.

But Sam didn't have the luxury of waiting for the expected midday thaw that would occur fourteen hours later, or even until daybreak. Her father's life hung in the balance, and she needed to be by his side. Besides, it wasn't like there was ready lodging in these parts. She'd passed the last motel an hour ago and the small, roadside gas stations, some of them housing country stores, all closed by nine p.m. Some even may have shuttered down earlier with word of the impending storm. Sam was glad she'd stopped to fill her gas tank when she had.

Sam viewed the rugged mountains in the distance. Soon she'd have to cross them, and the curves that were already starting to bend at the foothills' base would become even more daunting, the drop-offs beneath them precipitous. Sam tried not to think about that, and focused instead on the road ahead, tightening her fingers around the wheel. *One step at a time* was all she needed to conquer. In another two hours, she'd see the light her mother kept burning in the window at home.

Lisa replaced the small bulb in the short plastic candle in the front hall window. It was the sort that people put out at Christmastime. The year Sam's brother Jimmy went missing at sea was the year she'd left one candle out when she'd packed the rest of the Christmas decorations away. Affable and good-looking, Jimmy had possessed a natural way of charming the ladies—beginning with his kindergarten teacher, who had assured his parents Jimmy was destined to do great things. He'd grown up in a popular crowd, his friends coming and going throughout their busy household day after day. Jimmy played football and was a star swimmer. When he'd announced his desire to become a

Navy Seal, then won his scholarship to the U.S. Naval Academy, none of his teachers was surprised.

Jimmy had ambition and a plan, unlike his sister, who had talent yet no goals. Quiet and introspective like her father, Sam took longer to come into her own. She'd been a happy child with a few close friends, but didn't decide to pursue art professionally until college. There she'd met a photography professor she admired, and the rest was history. She'd made a wonderful career for herself, and Ben and Lisa couldn't have been more proud. If only Jimmy were around to see it.

Something raw caught in Lisa's throat and she drew in a sniff. They were never told exactly what had happened to Jimmy, only that he'd died bravely, serving his country. At times, thoughts of his death overwhelmed her. Mostly, Lisa forced herself not to think about it at all because the pain ran too deep.

She sank weakly into a living room chair, also thinking of Ben. Lisa wasn't sure how she could move forward without the two of them. Though Ben had promised her she would. "Be a good wife and bring me some Scotch," he'd said, dragging his thumb across her cheek. He'd caught a tear there, but pretended not to notice. "You'll be okay, hon. No matter what. You've got Sam." Yes, but Sam was a young woman with a life of her own, and Lisa would never interfere with that.

They'd been discussing Ben's condition, which seemed to be getting worse—even after triple-bypass surgery and his staying on medication. Lisa had been urging Ben to return to the doctor, but he kept putting it off, saying he would go just as soon as he got some important project wrapped up.

"You're not supposed to drink Scotch and you know it."

"Right." He gave her a wry smile, blue eyes dancing beneath a mop of silvery hair. "Could shave another fifteen minutes off at the end."

"Ben!" she said, aghast.

"Who says I'll even want those last fifteen minutes? They could be perfectly dreadful." Ben's illness hadn't deprived him of his sense of humor, or his looks. He still had a commanding presence and a handsome face. The fact that it was etched with wrinkles only made him look more seasoned, like a seafarer of sorts, or someone who'd weathered life's storms. Oh, how Lisa prayed he would weather this one. He pulled her out of her reverie with a quip.

"Better make mine a double."

She laughed lightly and fixed him his drink. Within minutes, she regretted that decision. The glass slipped from his hand, colliding with the carpet as he doubled forward, gripping his arm. In a flash, Lisa was on the phone dialing 9-1-1. The EMTs arrived quickly, then Ben was whisked away to the hospital in an ambulance.

After a quick consultation with his surgeon, he was being admitted to the hospital and prepped for emergency surgery. Another open-heart operation was risky, coming so close on the heels of his previous one. But at the moment, it was the only option they had. Lisa rushed home to gather Ben's things and place a few calls. She wondered if she'd been right in alerting Sam on such a treacherous night, though she sensed that her daughter never would have forgiven her if she hadn't.

Lisa stared out the window at the icy rain, knowing Sam was doing everything in her power to get home. Lisa had tried to dissuade her from traveling tonight, begging her to wait until tomorrow, when the roads would be clearer. But Sam wouldn't hear of it. She was her daddy's girl.

"Put your coat on and come with me, Sam."

Six-year-old Sam looked up at her dad, twin pigtails skimming each shoulder. She had honey-colored hair like her mom's, but her sky-blue eyes were her dad's. "Where are we going, Papa?" Her mom looked up from her knitting on the sofa, her raised brow asking the same question.

"To see some *magic*." He winked at his wife and Lisa laughed, apparently remembering something they'd shared earlier.

Sam eagerly slipped on her coat, sensing another adventure. Her dad was full of them. She especially loved adventuring with him at night. He worked for a big telescope lab and sometimes took trips to exotic-sounding places. Mostly, though, he worked remotely from the regional office nearby, which allowed him to do what he enjoyed most: spending time with his family. When Jimmy was younger, he liked these adventures too. Now that Jimmy was in high school and into sports and girls, things had changed. So it was often just Sam who accompanied Papa on his missions.

"Don't keep her out too late!" her mom cautioned as they slipped out the door. "School tomorrow!"

"One can't always predict the stars, my love."

"I beg to differ." Lisa smiled softly. "I seem to know a gentleman who can."

Ben gave a low chuckle, then tugged the door shut behind them, leading Sam toward the truck. "We're going to Barrett's Field?" she asked, excited by the possibilities. Only the most spectacular things happened there. Like when Sam witnessed her first meteor shower. Her dad had roused her at four in the morning for that one. Her mom really was a good sport. Even though she never wanted to come along, she seemed content to let Sam have fun.

An hour later, Sam shivered beneath the truck blanket as she sat on the edge of a haystack.

Her dad quit fiddling with his field telescope. "Too cold for you?" he asked with concern.

"Uh-uh," Sam lied, little puffs of breath hovering above her lips. She stared up at a bright object glittering like a diamond. "What's that one, Papa?"

"Polaris. The North Star." He smiled warmly. "If you ever get lost, it can help lead you home."

"How?"

"It's true north. Always has been, always will be."

Ben checked his watch, then adjusted the telescope, sharpening the focus of the lens. "Aha!"

Sam sucked in a breath, unable to bear the suspense. He hadn't told her what they'd come for, but it was bound to be big. Her father motioned her closer and she took her position before the scope. A grainy globe danced across her field of vision, in very slow motion as if it were swimming underwater. Only it was dragging something long behind it, shimmering and wonderful, like the train on her Aunt Beth's wedding dress. Sam had served as a flower girl just last year.

She pulled back from the eyepiece to catch her father wearing a broad grin. "You can even see it with the naked eye. Beautiful, isn't she?"

Sam stared into the rich, sparkly night sky studded with stars, and one gloriously dancing bride. "She looks just like Aunt Beth."

Ben chuckled aloud, getting it immediately. "A bride? Hmm." He thoughtfully stroked his chin. "I like that name for a comet, but this one already belongs to someone."

"What do you mean?"

"The astronomer who found her first got to name her."

"Wow."

She shot him a hopeful look. "Will you name something after me?"

He smiled and thumbed her nose. "Someday? Most certainly."

Moisture gathered in Sam's eyes as she recalled her dad's high-school graduation gift. Not only was he funding her attendance at a prestigious state university; he'd also presented her with something far more personal. He'd studied twin planets somewhere in a faraway galaxy. One had a previously undiscovered moon. Due to its fixed orbit, it stayed brightly illuminated at all times. He'd named it Sam's Bride. Her dad had joked that some day in the future, folks might speculate about a space explorer named Sam and admire his marital tribute, never knowing the true origin of the name.

Sam's back wheels slipped suddenly and she clutched the steering wheel as the anti-skid control mechanism kicked in. Heaving a breath, Sam decided she needed to pay more attention to her driving and less to her memories, but they were hard to put aside. An ache rose in her chest so fierce that it burned. Sam couldn't lose her dad now, she just couldn't. More tears pooled, blurring her vision for a fraction of a second too long. *No!* She quickly righted her path, steering her car back into the center of her lane. There was barely any shoulder here, and the terrain was getting steeper. Just a few more miles, and she'd be over this ridge.

Chapter Two

Jake Marlow normally wouldn't be driving this road tonight. However, a last-minute business emergency demanded it. His boss had asked him to go the extra mile as a personal favor. The friendship between him and this client was decades old. Under usual circumstances, Jake's boss would have made the trip himself, but his daughter was getting married this weekend at a destination wedding half the world away. Jake ran a hand through his short dark hair, studying the snarl of traffic on the highway before him. Vehicles had skidded off the road, while others had collided with each other trying to navigate the slick overpass ahead.

The scene was a mess; he'd been sitting here for nearly an hour. If he waited too much longer, he'd burn through the gas he'd bought for the journey, and there wasn't much promise of too many filling stations being open tonight. Jake knew this road from a long time back. He used to take it with his law school buddies when they broke away from the books and drove up into the mountains for fly-fishing. There was this way, which was faster, and then... Jake snapped his fingers at the recollection. Of course! Instead of going straight over the mountains using the highway, while trying to combat this interstate insanity, he could wind his way around them by taking lesser-known back roads.

Jake punched data into his phone's GPS, hoping he remembered correctly. When the destination bubble bloomed bright red on the screen, Jake sighed with relief. It looked simple enough on the little map, he thought, wheeling his SUV onto the shoulder. By the time this pileup was cleared, he'd be halfway to River Falls. Jake was grateful for his four-wheel drive as he skirted around the others, his right tires skimming a narrow ditch. There was a piercing scrape against the undercarriage, screeching like dragging metal. Jake gritted his teeth and surged ahead, something clanking against the shoulder behind him. In his rearview mirror he spied the twisted remnants of a length of rebar. Probably construction reinforcements that had fallen off the back of a truck. Jake's eyes scanned the dashboard, but all the indicator lights remained steady. He was lucky he hadn't lost a tire—or worse.

Frozen rain was coming down harder now, crusting up on his windshield. Soon it would morph into full-fledged sleet. Jake hoped a blizzard wasn't in store, but found that unlikely at this time of year. Late-season ice storms were more typical. Like the one he was experiencing now. The sooner Jake got where he was going, the sooner he could get off the road—and out of the elements. There! Just ahead, an exit sign glistened. The next thing he knew, Jake was climbing the off-ramp and headed away from highway lights.

The darkness before her seemed impenetrable. Sam couldn't recall the mountains ever looking this black. The streaking sleet didn't help. It pummeled her windshield, punctuating the rhythm of the wiper blades sweeping back and forth across the icy glass. She rounded a curve and her wheels slipped, causing Sam to brake unexpectedly. Tires squealed as the back end of her car fishtailed wildly, swaying first to the left and then to the right. The traction control warning lights flashed on and Sam's pulse kicked into overdrive. She tried to correct her trajectory, but the weight of the car fought back. She was skidding in the wrong direction, helplessly thrown toward a low guardrail. Sam didn't trust it to withstand the force of a collision.

The sky beyond loomed darker still: an inky pit, shrouded in billowing fog. She furiously tugged at the steering wheel, trying something—anything—to make her vehicle change its course. Time slowed as her car rocketed toward the precipice. Sam held her breath and mustered every ounce of strength her body could render. One final tug on the wheel and—*yank!*—the car flipped around, spinning like a top. The band of the guardrail whipped by, once, twice... *Wham!* The trunk of her car slammed the guardrail and airbags exploded outward as her car shot back across the road, straight toward a rocky wall. Sam punched the brake pedal to the floor and the car lurched then screeched to a halt. Sam gasped, her heart pounding. That's when she looked out the window and saw her car teetered at the mouth of a ravine, a dark cavernous hole lurking just beyond the shoulder.

Jake shone his flashlight down the road, once again finding nothing. Before he'd rounded this turn, he thought he'd seen a flicker of light, maybe two. Moisture beaded his slicker that was stiffening up in the cold. He must have torn his tires on that rebar after all. Both right tires had blown at exactly the same time, two miles down the road. He'd been able to steer his SUV onto the shoulder and to safety. Luckily for him, his blowout hadn't happened up here, where the incline was steeper and the shoulder virtually nonexistent. He'd considered waiting with his vehicle until morning, but had decided that getting to a working phone was a better plan. His cell couldn't pick up any service here. He hoped that if he kept walking, he might come within range of a tower. Failing that, he might come across a service station, or even a farmhouse. *Right.* Who was he kidding? You couldn't find any place more remote than this part of Virginia.

Jake shook the streaming water from his hood and trudged ahead, thinking that all roads led somewhere. Before he'd lost the GPS signal, it had appeared he was roughly thirty miles from the nearest town. That was a big distance to travel on foot, but if he kept moving, he'd get there eventually. If the fates were with him, he'd find help long before that. Jake brought himself up short, thinking he smelled something odd. Burning rubber? The beam of his flashlight panned the road. What appeared to be an oil slick glimmered, coating the asphalt. But it wasn't oil. It was ice. Black ice. And fifteen feet beyond that, he spied skid marks. Jake swallowed hard, searching the boundaries of the road. Nothing to the right but the side of a craggy mountain, spiking toward dark clouds. But to the left…?

Jake cautiously stepped around the black ice and approached the dented guardrail. Something had slammed against it pretty hard, but thankfully hadn't busted through. He scoured the valley below with his light, finding ridge after jagged ridge, dangerously rising like daggers and pointing skyward into the icy night. But no wreckage lay among them. Which had to mean the driver had managed to avert disaster and stay on the road. Jake mopped his brow, once again considering his close call. If he'd blown his tires on this curve, he wouldn't have had a chance of survival.

Just to be sure he wasn't missing anything, Jake scoured the area with his flashlight one last time. Nothing seemed out of the ordinary, besides that plume of fog rising from the ravine lining the inner lane. *Wait. That's not fog.* Jake's senses heightened, taking in the familiar scent. *Not fog...exhaust! And, oh no, not that...* Right when it registered with certainty that Jake also smelled smoke, he heard a woman's screams.

Chapter Three

"Help! Please help me!" The voice was decidedly female. Definitely panicked.

Jake scurried toward the right shoulder, the hood of his slicker flipping back as his boots slid on ice. He didn't feel the frozen pings against his brow and lashes. He was too caught up in the horror ahead. There was a small patch of grass coated in white, beyond it only dark shadows emitting smoke and fire.

Jake halted at the top of the gaping ravine, calculating a ten-foot drop. At its bottom sat a banged-up economy sedan, wedged sideways. Now, Jake smelled something worse than exhaust and smoke. *Gasoline.* Flames leapt from the engine, reaching out from beneath the crumpled hood. And the fire was spreading, sending noxious fumes rising in waves. "Down here!"

Jake glanced around quickly. If he was going to descend the steep slope, he'd need a way to get back up. There was the trunk of a skinny tree nearby. He grasped it firmly near its base and pulled with all his might. It bent and sagged forward under the strain, but didn't break. It was all he had, so he'd take it. The trouble was he'd never reach it from deep inside that gulley. What he needed was a rope. "Just sit tight!" he called for reassurance. "I'm coming!" Jake raked a hand through his hair, thinking fast. Of course! His belt. He unhitched it quickly and yanked it from the loops of his jeans. Fire sizzled as electrical wires popped. More black smoke rushed toward him. He'd have to hurry. "Can you hear me?" he called, his breath ragged.

Sam squinted up through the broken passenger window at the dark figure holding a flashlight and yelled an affirmative. The airbags had deflated, leaving her wedged against her driver's door in the tight constraint of her shoulder harness. Light flickered across the starburst pattern that had erupted on the windshield upon impact.

"How many of you are down there?"

"Just me! One!"

Sam felt light-headed and feverish. It occurred to her for the first time that this Good Samaritan might not be so altruistic. What if he was a madman? Somebody dangerous, with bad intentions? She hadn't seen flashing lights, or heard ambulance or police sirens. His face peered in at her, framed by shards of glass and followed by a bright beam of light. Sam blinked and instinctively withdrew against the door.

"You're hurt."

"No, I—"

He scanned the interior of the car, then settled on her face. "Your forehead, it's bleeding."

She touched a hand to her hairline and her fingers came away sticky. All at once Sam was aware of the gash on her head, which must have hit something when she was thrown forward. Or maybe she'd hit the steering wheel when the car tumbled over. Sam's stomach roiled and she feared she might get sick.

"Can you move your legs?" he asked, smoke coiling around him.

"Wh...what?"

"Kick your feet! Can you get them free?"

She did as he instructed, but everything ached. Her calves felt bruised, her ankles twisted. But she could move them, yes. "They don't feel pinned by anything."

"Good." He angled his flashlight to study the exterior of the car and set his lips in a determined line. The shadows revealed a rugged face with a sturdy jaw and solid cheekbones. "What's your name?"

"S...S...Sam," she stammered, her lips quivering. Tremors took hold of her torso, shaking it violently. "What's happening to me?"

Despite the direness of the situation, his voice remained steady. "I'm going to get you out of there, Sam. But you've got to trust me. Okay?"

A *kaboom* rocked the engine, sending flames spewing as the air clogged with suffocating smoke. Sam yelped. But the crackling only got louder, snapping and popping like a lit fuse racing toward a stack of dynamite. The windshield above her heaved and sagged, melting in the flames.

He tugged at the passenger side door, but couldn't get it open.

"Turn away!" the man instructed.

"What?" Sam had already wiggled out of her seatbelt and was preparing to flee.

"Now, Sam! Turn! Shield your face!"

She complied and he knocked in the window, sending shards flying onto the passenger seat. Using his heavy flashlight as a tool, Jake dislodged the remaining pieces of glass, then stretched an arm toward her. The smoke was growing thicker, clouding the inside of the car. Jake had to get her out before she inhaled it. Already, his lungs strained against the heavy fumes. Fortunately, Sam was upwind of their torrid assault, but she wouldn't be for long. At any second, the gas tank could blow, consuming them both in a massive explosion.

Sam cowered against the driver's door, shaking violently. But there wasn't much time. One more *kaboom* and they were both history. "Sam," Jake cried hoarsely, reaching for her.

Her head came around, honey-blond hair cascading past her shoulders. Tears streamed from her eyes that appeared oceans deep. He'd give anything to calm the sea storm within them. The best way he knew of was getting her out alive. "Take my hand!"

She shook her head, seemingly incoherent. Another loud boom sent a cloud of smoke curling in on a wave of heat. Jake shielded his mouth with a forearm and tried again. "Come on, you've got to work with me."

She was choking on the smoke now, her eyes clearly stinging. She dropped her head forward, resting it in her palms. Jake was losing her, but without Sam's cooperation they'd never make it. Metal wrenched and the car slid inches deeper into the ravine. He'd thought it had settled at the bottom, but he'd been wrong. If Jake didn't get them out now, the length of his belt wouldn't be enough to help them navigate the muddy slope before the burning car became a fireball. *Crackle...hiss...whine...*

He made one more attempt, pleading, "Sam, look at me."

When she did, he said, "There must be something you want to live for."

She blinked, then drew in a breath, grim reality apparently whipping into focus.

Then, in an instant, she lunged forward and gripped his hand.

Chapter Four

One hand was firmly seated in his, the other frantically grabbing his wrist. If Jake hadn't had his wits about him and been prepared for Sam's sudden surge of strength, she might have pulled him into the vehicle with her. "Easy," he cautioned, as he hoisted the top half of her body through the broken window. She removed her death-hold on his wrist and clamped an arm around his neck.

"I don't think I can—" She gulped a breath, the fire's glow lapping at her hair. Heat broiled around them, flames leaping taller.

"Oh yes, you can." He lifted the rest of her small frame up and through the window's opening.

She kicked with her loafers, trying to gain leverage against the car's side and assist him. Her shoes made purchase with the door and she pressed herself upward in an attempt to right herself. But the effort was too much. She fainted dead away in Jake's arms.

Jake stared down at the helpless woman and tightened his embrace. The fire burned hotter, enveloping them in thick black smoke. It was a matter of seconds now, not minutes. He'd looped his belt around the tree base and its end now hung a few inches out of reach.

Jake slid Sam over his shoulder, her hips pressing against it while her torso draped down his back. He pinned her legs to his chest with one arm, and stretched his other hand toward the belt. Nearly...*there.* His fingers found the leather strap and tightened around it. *Crackle, hiss, flare!* Jake squinted against the fire flash and centered his strength on his right arm. If he were to save them, he'd have to move *now!*

Then he was scrambling up the hill.

Jake hit the embankment panting and raced from the ravine at top speed with Sam cradled in his arms. Before he reached his destination—a broad oak with sprawling limbs—a fireball exploded at his back. Its force sent him stumbling forward, but he managed to stay upright on quaking knees and drew Sam against his chest. Jake ran for shelter, his pulse pounding, as flaming debris jettisoned through the air and spiked into the ground around him. Finally, the fury ceased and the air went dark just as Jake reached the tree. It was only then that he realized the sleet had stopped.

Sam awoke to bone-chilling cold, a smoky haze filling the air. But her cheek and the right side of her body were warm. She observed the oversized rain jacket that had been laid spread-eagle on top of her, then slowly scanned a set of outstretched legs. They were covered in muddied jeans that brushed the tops of worn hiking boots. She heard heavy breathing, the sound of somebody sleeping beside her. Then, Sam remembered.

Raising her chin, she encountered a handsome face, almost entirely shrouded in shadows. Soft light streamed through gnarled branches, illuminating his solid frame. He was tall, probably over six feet, with a muscled chest and arms, one wrapped firmly around her, holding her in place. The gray sweatshirt, against which she'd been resting, read *U.S. Navy.* Immediately, she thought of Jimmy. Then of her dad. *I have to get home.* She tried to pull away, but her head felt too heavy.

"Careful."

Sam looked up into ebony eyes that had opened. They surveyed her carefully, worry lines deepening around them. "You don't want to move too quickly. You took quite a blow to your head." Beyond him, clouds ringed the moon, giving it an eerie halo.

"Where are we?" Her voice warbled.

He smiled calmly, in stark contrast with the calamity of their situation. "Virginia."

"Yes, but where…?" Sam blinked hard and took another look around. The remnants of smoke coiled from the lip of a faraway ravine. "My car!"

"I'm afraid it's gone."

She turned desperately to face him. "My cell? My *camera?*"

He shook his head.

Sam sucked in a breath. "We're stranded, aren't we?"

"I wouldn't exactly say *stranded.* Someone could happen by."

"And if they don't?"

"We'll devise a plan."

Sam's head throbbed and her whole body ached, but she couldn't leave things up to chance. "What about your car?"

"It's not in as bad shape as yours, but it's not running either. Lost two tires a few miles back. I've only got one spare."

A chill enveloped her and Sam shivered.

"We should probably get you off this wet ground," he said. "Do you think you can stand?"

Sam carefully set aside the slicker and unsteadily got to her feet.

He followed her movements and stood as well, his hands outstretched to catch her if necessary. "Just give yourself a minute," he cautioned.

She nodded and inhaled deeply, feeling a slight pinch in her side as she got her balance. Finally, the world stopped spinning and things came into focus. Including the great-looking guy standing beside her. He reached out and gently cupped her elbow. "Doing okay?"

Sam smiled weakly. "Better. It just took a moment to get my bearings." It was impossible for Sam to tell how much time had elapsed since her accident. Eons seemed to have slipped away. "How long was I out?"

"I drifted off for a while too," he admitted before checking his cell. The man frowned when he saw its face was cracked, moisture beading the screen on the inside. He tried navigating with his finger, then punched a few buttons, but to no avail. The display was frozen. Stopped dead at ten forty-seven.

Sam stared at his phone then read his expression.

"Sorry, we're out of luck." He slid the useless phone into his pocket with a silent curse. Sam surmised he'd damaged it somehow when he'd pulled her from her car. He checked the angle of the moon before answering her earlier question. "It's been about two hours. I'd guess more than two hours since I found you."

Two hours? That was a lot of time to spend on the frigid ground. No wonder Sam's limbs felt frozen through and her veins ran icy cold.

The man stepped back, assessing her. "How do your legs feel when you move? Your arms and hands?"

She tested them all, flexing her fingers, and they seemed fine. Though her left ankle hurt a little. "Not too bad, considering."

He surveyed her again from head to toe. "It doesn't appear anything's broken."

"Are you a doctor?"

"Lawyer."

"Oh!" Sam couldn't hide her surprise. "I wouldn't have guessed that." Sam wasn't about to tell him that her impression of lawyers at the moment was very negative, owing to the fact that an entire firm was trying to force her group of artists out of business. Some hotshot businessman had his eye on her studio and several other properties in the arts district. He planned to raze them all and put up a spanking new multiplex, complete with a food court selling cheeseburgers. He'd hired a team of attorneys to assist him with his takeover. They were looking for loopholes in the artists' current lease agreements so they could force them out.

"Okay, bring it on," the guy said. "If you've got a good lawyer joke, I've probably heard it. Might even have told it myself."

"I'm sorry. That didn't come out right. What I meant was—"

A smile teased the corner of his lips. "Not all of us in the profession are viewed as gallant knights, but I promise you I'm not one of the bad guys."

Somehow Sam didn't doubt that. He'd done nothing but prove himself honorable in the limited time she'd known him. Still, she ventured to ask, "Not in real estate law, I hope?"

He sputtered a laugh. "Not even close." He gently took her arm in his hand. "Mind if I check your pulse?"

"Beg pardon?"

"I'd like to make sure your standing right now is a good idea."

"So you *do* have medical training."

He slightly raised her sleeve and brought his fingers to her pulse point. "Military training."

"Ah." She focused on his sweatshirt as her pulse thudded under his fingers. He seemed to be counting in his head. "U.S. Navy."

"Guilty. But not anymore."

Sam raised her brow, not understanding.

He released her wrist with a smile, indicating he was satisfied. Apparently, she wasn't in danger of dying just yet. "I *was* in the Navy. Now I'm a gosh-darned civilian."

Sam massaged her wrist where he'd held it, feeling as if it sparked with electricity. How long had it been since she'd felt any chemistry with a man? A few years? Maybe five? "What made you get out?"

His deep laugh rumbled. "Your mind's working very clearly, I see."

"Meaning, you don't want to talk about it."

He shrugged, and it occurred to Sam that she didn't even know his name.

As if reading her mind, he held out his hand.

"Jake Marlow. Nice to meet you."

"I'd say the pleasure is much more mine." He locked on her eyes and Sam felt herself blush, hoping he couldn't see this in the moonlight. "You *did* save me." A new shiver took hold and Sam wrapped her arms around herself for warmth.

"If you believe you can walk, it might be good for us to get going." He glanced at the moon, which danced in and out of clouds. "Before more bad weather sets in. I think we're better off moving than staying put. At least our blood will be circulating."

"What are we close to?"

"Not much in the way of civilization. But I'm hoping we'll come across a farmhouse somewhere."

Jake pulled his slicker off the ground and fished a flashlight from the pocket before handing the jacket to Sam. "You might want to put this on."

"But the sleet has stopped."

"For an extra layer of warmth."

"What about you?"

"Some say I hold enough hot air to float a balloon."

Sam pressed her lips together to avoid giggling. "Now you're talking crazy."

He cracked a grin. "Maybe. But it worked. I almost got you to smile."

"Pretty impressive."

Nope, Jake decided. Sam was the impressive one. Here was a woman who'd barely escaped death and she'd come back kicking. Even with that cut marring her forehead, she was a beauty.

Sam slipped into his slicker and it engulfed her petite form. "Which way?" she asked, yanking up the zipper.

Jake clicked on his flashlight and swept the borders of the road. "I can tell you there's nothing doing in the direction I came from. Probably best to forge ahead." Jake met her eyes and a pinprick of recognition pierced him, but he brushed it off as irrational. Jake was certain he'd never met Sam. If he had, it would have been impossible to forget her. "How well do you know this road?"

"Not well at all," she admitted. "I haven't taken it in a long time."

"That makes two of us."

Chapter Five

While they walked, Sam told Jake about her father. Without supplying any details, she created a rough sketch of a man who was very ill and might not make it until morning. Sam had already lost her brother and she was the only child her dad had left. She was also the sole support for her mother, whose parents had died some years ago. Jake's chest ached for Sam and the weight she was under. His trip involved someone who was critically ill, as well. The difference was, in his case, it was *business.* For Sam, this was personal.

Jake was grateful Sam had escaped her accident with only minor injuries. He couldn't imagine how devastating it might be for her family had she been seriously hurt.

"I'm sorry for everything you're going through," he told her. "I wish there was a way that I could help."

"You already are helping. It's hard to think, but I..." She turned away, unable to meet his eyes and face the truth at the same time. She continued softly, speaking over her shoulder. "I might not even be here without you."

"I'm just glad I was in the right place at the right time."

When he'd first laid eyes on Sam's car, Jake feared it was hopeless. Then his old military training kicked in, along with his die-hard spirit. He didn't even remember half of what happened. He only knew two things for sure: He had gotten Sam out alive, and he had inhaled a lot of smoke. Not that he wouldn't make the same sacrifice again, but his lungs had taken a beating in the process. His insides felt like the creosote lining a chimney.

Sam stopped suddenly, a cramp evidently piercing her side. She bent forward, resting her hands on her thighs.

Jake worried that he was pushing her too hard. "You all right?"

She let out a long huff, then sucked in more air. "Guess I'm in worse shape than I thought."

"It's not that," he protested kindly. "It's what you've been through. Kind of knocked the wind out of me too." He drew a cleansing breath, but it didn't help much. His chest constricted and burned as he released a wheezing cough.

She straightened slowly, then eyed him from top to bottom, surveying his damp clothing. "Your accident?" she asked. "Was it as bad as mine?"

"It was no fun, I can tell you that. But it was hardly the picnic you went through."

"I wouldn't exactly call it a picnic."

Jake ran a hand through his hair, considering this. "No, it was more like a barbecue," he couldn't help but say.

His unexpected humor caught her off guard. "Jake!" She swatted a hand in his direction, but somehow she was laughing. Then her mouth took a downward turn.

A frown worked the corners of his mouth. "Hey. Why so grim?"

"Why?" Sam swept her arm over the landscape. "This! Just look around! There's no—" Sam stopped short at Jake's cry of surprise.

"Sam! Look!" He saw two beams of light, like headlights painting the road. Their aura glowed, then merged in the distance.

Sam started running in that direction, but Jake grabbed her by the arm and held her back. "Easy. We don't know what's out there."

"Of course we do! A car! Or maybe a truck!"

"Sam," he said, his voice low. "Then it's driving on the wrong side of the road."

Worry lines creased her forehead. "Drunk?"

"Let's hope not." Jake motioned for her to stay behind him as he stuck to the shoulder. There was a sharp turn ahead of them that blocked their view. "Could be just having trouble on the ice."

"What do you plan to do?" Sam queried.

"As soon as we get a clear view of him and I'm certain he can see us, I'll wave this"—he raised his flashlight—"and flag him down."

Jake's heart pounded. Thank goodness a rescue was imminent. For a while he'd been concerned they'd be stuck out here all night. Jake couldn't see the light anymore, but reasoned it would reappear the moment they fully made their way around this curve. But when they got to the other side, it was gone.

"I know I saw something," Sam said. "I didn't imagine it."

Jake used his flashlight to scan the shadows. "Nothing there now."

"Then what could have—?"

"Maybe a truck or an SUV with high beams?"

"That just disappeared?"

"No, that's unlikely. More probable it turned off somewhere. Maybe down a driveway or side road we can't see from here."

Of course, Jake was right. There had to be a logical explanation.

"The good news is," he continued, "we're not as alone out here as we thought. If we spotted one vehicle along this route, we're bound to see another, or at least get a better clue as to where that first one went."

Sam took a deep breath, releasing her tension. "Yes."

"Let's keep going," he urged, leading the way.

But as they progressed down the road, they didn't come to a driveway…or a turnoff…or anything. Jake decided it was best to ignore that detail rather than belabor it. Who knew what they'd seen? Might have even been a glimmer of moonlight, or their eyes playing tricks on them. He sure wasn't going to stir things up further by starting to speculate, when it was far better to stay focused on their goal.

He glanced at the woman walking behind him. Sam smiled bravely, but worry marred her features. "We're going to be all right, you know," he told her. "We'll get to help sooner or later." If only he believed it. But inwardly his conviction wavered. Although she claimed to be fine, Sam had hit her head and required medical attention. They both needed a change of clothes, or they would catch their death of cold. Jake's skin felt as clammy as a fish's underbelly, though he wouldn't admit this to Sam. *I'm tough enough to shake off a little cold.* Jake noted the fingertips of the hand that gripped his flashlight were turning blue. *But maybe not indefinitely.* They needed to move a little more quickly to keep their blood pumping.

Her voice rose in a plea behind him. "Can we please slow down?"

He turned to find her huffing and puffing, once again challenged by their brisk pace. But Jake's instincts said they shouldn't slow down. The wind was picking up and the temperature was dropping. What's more, the sky was clouding over, threatening more bad weather. They needed to find shelter, and soon.

"Do you think you can make it a little farther?" he asked her. "If we don't come to something shortly, we'll stop and rest."

She nodded her agreement and soldiered on. Jake hoped he was doing the right thing, but what other choice did he have? Even though he could strike out on his own and send back help, he'd never leave Sam out here alone. Jake wasn't the type to leave folks behind. Except for when the cruel fates dictated it.

Chapter Six

The wind kicked up, sending spooky howls echoing off the mountains. Though it was freezing out, Sam had to admit Jake was right about moving quickly helping them stay warm. Perhaps warm was an overstatement. Sam's feet had turned to blocks of ice within her leather loafers and her fingertips felt like frozen popsicles. She withdrew them from the flimsy pockets of Jake's rain slicker to massage them after vigorously rubbing her palms together.

"I know it seems bad," he called above the wind. Tree limbs rustled, new buds coated in dripping ice. "But we're making progress."

Yeah, toward where? Sam wondered if they'd made a mistake by heading forward into unknown terrain, rather than returning to the highway where they might be more prone to get help. State troopers were surely patrolling the main roads and searching for vehicles that had become disabled in the storm. Who knew what they would find in this direction, if anything at all?

Sam didn't want to sound ungrateful for his assistance. After all, she might not even *be here* without him. Still, her doubts were growing by the minute. The more they forged ahead, the more distant they became from the highway, and the more removed from a safe rescue the two of them might be. "Do you think we should have gone the other way?"

"No, and I'm certain."

"What makes you so sure?"

Dense fog rose off the road in a cloaking mist. Jake's flashlight beam pierced it. "That, right there."

Sam swallowed hard, not daring to believe it. Either this was some sort of crazy mirage, or—

"A diner," Jake announced, his flashlight trained on the purple neon sign.

Before he could comment further, Sam was racing through the haze toward the low brick building. Becky's Diner sat like a double-wide trailer in an empty parking lot, its windows fogged from the inside. Jake caught up with Sam just as she pulled back the door. A wave of warmth enveloped them as door chimes jangled, and the lights were oh-so-bright. Sam sucked in a wheeze, her right side pinching.

A woman wearing an apron approached with a welcoming smile. "Hey y'all, my name's Becky. I'll be taking care of—" Her gray eyes widened, crow's-feet deepening around them. "Goodness gracious! Just look at you two! You're soaked."

Jake shot Becky a humble grin. "Might say we've had dryer days."

Sam didn't want to be rude but she couldn't waste time on chitchat. Her mom was probably worried, and she had to get home to her dad. "Do you have a phone we could use?"

Becky's forehead wrinkled beneath the bangs of her wispy short hair. It was light brown and layered in a style that had been popular decades ago. "In here, hon?" She glanced around the diner, motioning to the row of vacant booths and the unoccupied stools at the counter. There didn't appear to be another employee or customer in sight. "Not much chance of that."

"We've had car trouble," Jake explained.

"My car hit black ice," Sam filled in. "If it hadn't been for Jake..." She glanced at him, then addressed Becky. "Suffice it to say, he may have saved my life."

Becky studied them with sympathy. "I'm sorry to hear you've had such a rough time. Those roads are darn near impassable." She sighed, apology in her eyes. "The truth is the storm took down our phone lines. Landline, that is. Went out today midafternoon. My boss called my cell phone to warn me."

"Cell?" Jake asked hopefully. "Do you think we might use it?"

Becky sadly shook her head. "Left it back in Darryl's truck.

Sam's heart plummeted and her stomach filled with lead. "Darryl?"

"He's my boyfriend. Dropped me off here 'bout an hour ago. Normally, I wouldn't have come in. But the boss said I might be needed. Never know when someone might..." She stopped talking and surveyed them up and down. "Just listen to me yapping my head off while the two of you are freezing to death."

Sam shivered unexpectedly and hugged her arms at the elbows, the fabric of Jake's slicker crinkling as she did.

Jake turned to Becky, his damp Navy sweatshirt molded to his broad chest. "I don't suppose you'd know where we could get some dry clothes?"

Becky's face brightened. "As a matter of fact, I do." She motioned for them to follow her through the swinging door to the kitchen.

Sam glanced at Jake, who raised an eyebrow. "After you," he said, stepping aside.

Becky hauled two large plastic leaf bags from a storeroom at the back of the kitchen, dragging them across the floor. "Diner holds an annual Spring Cleaning Drive each April. We collect these for local charities." She smiled warmly. "Y'all look in as bad a need of charity as any folks I've seen." Becky untied the topknot on one of the bags and opened it wide, splaying its sides apart with her fingers. "Ought to be something to fit you in here."

Sam stared into the dark space at the neatly folded garments arranged in stacks.

"All nice and laundered," Becky said. "Don't take 'em any other way."

"Wow," Sam replied. "What a gold mine."

"Yeah." Becky slid a bag toward Jake. "Why don't we get your fellow to haul these *bags of gold* into the restroom, where you two can change?"

Jake blinked and Sam's face flamed. "Oh, no! He's not my... What I mean is—"

Becky took a moment to scrutinize them both. "I'm sorry. I just assumed. What with the two of you coming in together." She turned to Jake. "Didn't she say you were her hero of the—?"

Was it Sam's imagination or did Jake's neck color slightly above the collar of his sweatshirt? "Hardly a hero, ma'am." He gave a self-effacing laugh. "What she meant was that I helped her out of a tight spot. It was Sam's car that hit the ice. My SUV blew two tires several miles back."

Becky's chin puckered in a frown. "Well, you kids sure have had your run of bad luck."

Sam heaved a sigh. "We're just lucky we found you."

"Sam's got that right." Jake lifted a bag in one arm and threw the other over his shoulder. He shot Becky a grateful smile. "Why don't you point us in the direction of that restroom?" Noting Sam was starting to color again, he quickly added, "We'll take turns."

On her fourth try, Sam found a pair of women's jeans that fit, and a heavy sweater too. Since they were supposedly moving into the warmer months, folks were obviously discarding winter clothing. She rummaged in the second bag until she found a passable pair of ladies' underwear and some funky knee socks. Her own undergarments had been soaked through. It was no wonder, considering all the time she and Jake had spent on the soggy ground under that tree. When she'd awakened, she'd found herself in Jake's arms with his rain slicker draped over her like a blanket. Gratitude flooded her. *I owe Jake more than mere thanks.* Sam thought of the burning car. *I owe him my life.*

Sam changed quickly on the cold bathroom tile, then dared to approach the mirror. She startled at her reflection: the tangled mass of hair…that angry gash at her hairline…and her skin was ghostly pale. She turned on the hot water spigot, thinking to wash up and cleanse her head wound with soap from the metal dispenser hanging over the sink. Maybe she'd even bring some color back into her cheeks.

Her face warmed beneath the soapsuds as she recalled how rapidly she'd blushed at Becky's insinuation that Jake was her boyfriend. Not that she'd mind having a boyfriend who looked like Jake. Meaning, if she were ever in the market. Not that she was. Despite her dad's mistaken notion that she was the toast of the town, Sam really hadn't had many successes in the dating department. She hadn't been dating lately at all. Mostly, she hung out with mixed groups, or had occasional lunches with girlfriends. Sam had spent these past five years building her business, and establishing the gallery had been hard work. Hard work was good because it helped take her mind off of other things. Like how quickly a relationship could go south.

Sam ran the water cold and splashed off the last of the soap, dabbing her face and neck with paper towels. The cut had stopped bleeding, and it looked a little less fearsome. She'd ask Becky about a first aid kit, so she could apply a dab of antibiotic cream and cover it with a bandage. But first, she had to decide what to do with her old clothes. Sam scanned the sterile room, her eyes landing on a tall waste bin. *There's no saving these now,* she thought, scooping her soggy rags off the floor. Apart from being wet, they were caked with mud and soot. Even worse, they were tainted with an awful memory.

Without further thought, she dumped them in the trash and spun back toward the mirror, running her fingers through her hair. *There! That's better! Practically human.* Now that Sam was gathering her wits about her, she decided to ask Becky when her boyfriend would be returning. It would probably be at the end of Becky's shift; then she and Jake would have a way to call for help. *Of course!* That's when it hit her. The lights that she and Jake had seen up ahead on the road...

She pried open the bathroom door to find Jake standing there, his whole face lit up. "It was Darryl!" he cried. "Those lights that we—"

"I know! I just put it together myself."

"When he gets back, we can—"

"My thoughts exactly."

Jake grinned. "Do you always finish other people's sentences?"

"Not usually." Then again, *usually* Sam wasn't so excited—or relieved—to learn she wasn't a nutcase. She hadn't been imagining things at all. Neither had Jake.

He gave her a satisfied perusal. "You clean up well. Feeling better?"

"Much." Sam started to exit the small restroom when she noticed Jake holding a first aid kit.

"From Becky," he said with a smile. His eyes were a deep chocolate brown and mesmerizing. They were the kind of eyes a woman could get lost in if she wasn't careful. But Sam needed to be careful, and stay focused on her goal, her goal of getting home. He nodded at her forehead then over to a stool by the counter. "Want to sit and let me have a look at that?"

"Oh no, it's all right," she said, taking the box from him. "I'll do it!" Then she darted back into the restroom and away from his curious gaze.

Chapter Seven

Jake slid into a booth by the front window, opposite Sam. He'd noticed from the start she was an attractive woman. Now, viewing her in the plain light of the diner, he found her beauty was even more apparent. She had the most stunning blue eyes that were the color of heaven, at least as he imagined it to be. Jake wondered briefly if she was some kind of angel, brought into his life for a purpose. Then he dismissed the notion just as quickly, questioning whether he too had taken a blow to the head. It wasn't like him to be superstitious or search out serendipitous meaning. His discovering Sam's wreck had been a lucky coincidence, but clearly not a happy one. He'd done his part in helping her just as he would have come to anyone's aid, because his training and instinct demanded it. There was nothing more to his involvement with Sam beyond that.

Becky arrived with a tray and set two steaming cups of coffee and a couple of glasses of water before them. "Creamer's on the table."

Sam gave Becky a grateful smile and took a sip from her cup. She apparently took hers black. "Mmm, delicious. Thanks."

Jake reached for the creamer and dumped a few
packets into his cup before addressing the waitress.
"Sam and I were wondering about Darryl?"

"Yes," Sam inserted. "About when he'll get back?"

"Since you left your cell in his truck—" Jake
started.

Becky stopped him by holding up a hand. "Won't
be back till morning, darlin'."

"Tomorrow?" Sam asked with dismay.

Becky smacked her gum. "That's when he returns
from his job. Running lumber over the mountain."

Jake studied the waitress with surprise. "You mean
to stay here all night?"

Becky motioned with her chin to the flashing neon
sign affixed to the window. "Open twenty-four hours."

Jake and Sam exchanged looks.

"Seems a lot for you to take on solo," Jake said.
"Without even the benefit of a cook."

Becky shrugged. "He'll be along soon enough."
She leaned forward with a whisper, even though there
was no one else around to hear her. "Once he gets his
wife to let him go."

"Wife?" asked Sam.

"Never did like his hours," Becky confided.
"'Specially doesn't like him traveling when the
weather's bad. But it pays the bills." The gum smacked
around her mouth a couple more times. "Know what
I'm saying?" She pulled an order pad from her apron
and eyed them both. "While we're waiting on Leroy to
arrive and fix you something proper, can I get you a
treat to go with that coffee? Maybe a piece of
homemade pie?"

Sam sighed softly. "What we'd really like is a telephone. My mom's waiting on me. I'm sure she'll be worried."

"I've got someplace to be too," Jake added, without giving too much away. Sam obviously had enough on her mind with her worries. No point in troubling her with his. There was only so much he could share anyway.

Becky stared out the window at the impenetrable fog, seeming to weigh something. "Well, there *is* Miss Beulah's place," she told them.

Sam looked up, long blond hair swinging over her shoulder. "But I thought you said all the landlines were down?"

"Her daughter's some high-falutin' doctor. Bought her one of those fancified phones a few years back, precisely for this reason. Unpredictable weather. Though I'm not sure she ever figured out how to use it." Becky smiled. "That don't work, you might try her ham radio. You can bet your bottom dollar she keeps that in working order."

Sam wore a hopeful expression. "How far away does she live?"

"'Bout a mile or so up the road. Just east of here." She motioned to the right. "You head up to the T intersection, then head that-a-way."

"How will we know her house?" Jake asked.

"Round here, aren't too many others like it. 'Sides that, she always keeps a light on."

Jake and Sam thanked Becky for the information, as well as her kind assurances that Miss Beulah wouldn't mind being troubled by two strangers this late at night. *Got a heart of gold, that one does,* she said.

Before they left, Becky insisted they have a little something to eat. She served them each a generous slice of hot apple pie, topped with whipped cream.

"This is really good," Sam said, digging in again with her fork. "I didn't realize how famished I was."

Jake nodded and sipped his coffee. "Guess we were both in need of some sustenance."

Sam drained her cup, then rubbed the tops of her arms through her sweater sleeves. "My veins are finally warming up. I'd swear they'd run ice-cold."

"How's the side?"

She set down her cup. "Side?"

"You seemed to have a stitch when we were walking."

Sam flattened the fingers of her right hand against her ribcage. "You're right," she said, sounding somewhat puzzled. "It was really bothering me before."

"And now?"

Sam met his gaze and Jake felt a jolt. It was like a lightning bolt of recognition. Or…something somehow familiar. It was the same sensation he'd had when speaking to Sam on the road earlier.

Pretty blue eyes warmed under his perusal. "Now I'm feeling much better, thanks. I guess it was the cold, or the walk. I was having trouble catching my breath."

"Have we met?" Jake asked her suddenly.

Sam appeared taken aback.

"I don't think so. I mean, I know so." Her cheeks turned pink. "I would have remembered you."

He grinned at the compliment and Sam felt her heart skip a beat. Maybe it was silly, but she felt as if she knew him too. Either that, or like she was destined to know him. Sam wondered how many women he'd rescued before, or whether she was his first.

She settled back against the booth and asked him, attempting to sound casual. "So. Is saving damsels in distress a regular line of work, or is that mostly a sideline?"

He gave a low chuckle. "I'd say it's more of a sideline. My day job is much more mundane than that."

"You said you're a lawyer?"

"Patent attorney."

"But not for the Navy?" she asked, recalling what he'd said before about getting out.

"Not anymore. Went through their student program in town."

"Meaning?"

"The Navy put me through law school, then I owed them some time." He thanked Becky, who came over to refill their cups.

Becky sent Sam a look intimating she sensed something brewing between her and Jake, but Sam ignored the sly glance. "And you served it," Sam said, once Becky had gone.

Jake lifted a shoulder. "Two tours of duty were enough for me."

"Where did they send you?"

"Washington, DC, and Iraq."

"Washington, I can see. But Iraq?"

"There was a war on. They needed every able body." His dark eyes grew somber. "Plus, I'm well versed in more than patent law."

"What else did you specialize in?"

"Estate planning, wills and…"

She felt a sting in her eyes and his voice trailed off.

"I'm sorry, Sam. I shouldn't have… What I mean is, I know how worried you must be about your father."

He met her eyes with compassion. "Has he been ill long?"

Sam lifted a paper napkin to dab the corner of her eye. "On and off for a couple of years. But lately…" Her voice faltered.

Jake reached across the table and laid a hand on her arm. "It's okay. You don't have to talk about it."

She pursed her lips for a beat before speaking. "It's all right. It was nice of you to ask."

"How about you?" he ventured, changing the subject. "How do you earn your bread and butter?"

Sam felt her mood lightening. They'd agreed to stay and finish a second cup of coffee before making their way up the road. It promised to be a long night. "I'm a photographer," she said proudly. "I have a whole black-and-white series featuring the valley. I don't know if you've seen it? Some of my work hangs in the restaurants in downtown Charlottesville."

"Charlottesville? No kidding!" His face lit up. "Like at the Mud Shop?" Jake asked, referring to the coffeehouse.

"Why yes! There and also at—"

"That Cuban place." Jake grinned from ear to ear.

"Wait a minute." Her jaw dropped slightly. "Are you saying you're from C'ville too?"

He nodded his assent and Sam's pulse pounded. How could she have missed seeing him there all this time? One thing was certain, she'd never miss spotting him again.

"I *have* seen your work," he continued. "It's fantastic. I even inquired about buying a piece."

Sam blushed. "Really? Which one?"

"I believe it was called *River Falls*. I asked for the artist's card, but the manager said he'd run out. Besides, that particular print had already sold." He shook his head, slightly bemused by this. "A little ironic, considering."

"Considering what?"

He met her eyes. "That's where I'm headed tonight."

Chapter Eight

Sam and Jake thanked Becky profusely for her generosity. Jake even offered to pay for their food and the change of clothing. "Don't be silly!" Becky said. "Both are on the house." Becky only regretted she didn't have any jackets to offer them to take along, so she'd insisted they each put on an extra sweater. Not that they really needed one. Now that they'd dried out, the cold didn't feel so biting. Perhaps the chill was lifting, or maybe they were both still wrapped in a blanket of warmth from having been indoors. Besides, Miss Beulah's was only a little ways up the road. Surely they'd cover that distance in no time, then they could simply wait there until help arrived. While Sam's car was a total loss, Jake was pretty sure he could get the SUV back in commission with relative ease. All he needed were two new tires and an auto service to give him a ride to where the vehicle had become disabled.

"Once I get that straightened out," he told Sam as they walked along, "I'll be glad to give you a lift to where you're going."

"I couldn't put you to the trouble. Not after all you've done."

"But I've already told you I'm headed to River Falls."

"Strange, isn't it? That we live in the same university town and were traveling to the same place?"

"A little." He used his flashlight to survey a field abutting the road. "Then again, this particular back road doesn't lead to too many places."

"And to only one hospital," she agreed.

That was precisely Jake's target destination. His boss's best friend was on the brink of making an important discovery. He was also seriously ill. He needed someone well versed in both patent law and estate planning to secure his interest in any profits and draft an amendment to his will. Should his invention hit as big as he imagined, his family could stand to benefit. But not if everything hadn't been taken care of properly from a legal standpoint first.

Sam eyed him curiously. "What's the name of your client? River Falls is in a small area. If he or she lives around there, I'm sure—"

"I'm afraid the particulars are confidential."

Sky-blue eyes searched his, and Jake was stung once again with a sense of déjà vu. "If they weren't, you'd tell me?"

"Of course." The sky started to spit again with icy spikes that plummeted from above. That's when Jake remembered. "My slicker!" he exclaimed. "I left it back at the diner." Jake mentally kicked himself for the sloppy oversight. There was no room for mistakes now, not when another soul depended on him.

"We haven't gone that far," Sam said. "Maybe we should turn around."

"We should definitely turn around," Jake said. "My keys are in the pocket."

They doubled back quickly, not wanting to lose more time. Jake was right in his reasoning about the SUV. Getting that up and running was their best chance of reaching River Falls before morning. There were certainly no cab services out here, and very few domiciles. Sam had been relieved to learn of Miss Beulah's farm. Most of this land lay in a protected national forest, and construction of any kind was strictly prohibited. Only a handful of small properties had been grandfathered in when the National Park Service took over. If Sam hadn't seen it herself, she wouldn't have believed they'd allowed a diner. Though she supposed even tourists and passers-through had to eat somewhere.

Jake trudged ahead, walking even faster than before, his flashlight beam trained on the road.

"Jake! Slow down!" Sam called, her side starting to pinch again. She couldn't fathom why he was moving so urgently. Surely, Becky was trustworthy enough to leave the rain jacket in her care for just a brief while.

"I can't." Jake set his jaw, his eyes fixed on the road ahead. "Not until I find it."

Sam huffed and puffed behind him, scurrying to catch up. "Find what?"

He spoke over his shoulder, but didn't turn to look at her. "Becky's Diner."

Sam could have sworn they hadn't covered this much distance going toward Miss Beulah's already. It seemed like they'd doubled back twice as far. "How much farther?" she asked panting.

Jake stopped and stood stock-still. A snakelike black road dissected two mountain ridges ahead of them. "We should have reached it a half mile ago."

Chapter Nine

Sam's heart hammered harder. "What do you mean we should have reached it a half mile ago?"

Jake angled his body toward hers, shadows framing his face. "What I mean is, I don't know where it is." He drew a breath. "It's gone."

"Gone? But that's imposs…" Sam searched the bleak landscape.

A full moon cut in and out of the clouds above, and fog billowed around them.

"I know it seems crazy." Jake ran a hand through his hair. "We've retraced our steps exactly."

"Maybe we took a wrong turn, or missed it in the fog? It's everywhere. I've never seen it this thick."

"Maybe it's the altitude, the damp mountain air." He tilted his chin toward the mountain pass. A glimmer of light shone from beyond it. "Look, Sam, over there."

The fog parted, exposing precipitous ledges punctuated by boulders on either side. "We…didn't come through anything like that."

"Could be the fog cloaked it," he said, motioning her ahead.

Sam took a step forward, then stumbled, losing her footing on the narrow shoulder. "Jake!"

He spun to catch her, shoring her up against him. All at once she was in his arms, her body pressed to his. Heat streaked across her cheeks and raced to her temples. She'd never known anyone like Jake: a confident man who looked after her. Her last boyfriend, Nelson, had been very needy. Insecure in his work and in himself, he'd repeatedly taken his inner disappointments out on Sam, until the day she decided she wouldn't tolerate one more angry outburst. By contrast, Jake was steady and reassuring…compassionate and kind. Plus, he had dark-brown eyes to die for.

"Are you all right?" he asked huskily.

"Yes. It's just that my ankle caught, and turned." She tested it, then grimaced and sagged in his embrace. He steadied her against his chest and she could feel his heart beating, its cadence lending rhythm to her own ragged breath.

His whiskey-smooth words warmed her. "You'll have to let me look at that."

Her pulse quickened as his head dipped lower and the heat of his mouth closed in. Sam felt herself longing for his kiss, because instinct said that one kiss from Jake could make the world and its troubles melt away.

Her lips parted in a whisper. "What's happening to us?"

"I don't know." His eyes searched hers. "But I intend to find out."

To her chagrin, he turned away to shine his flashlight across the road. "Do you think you can make it to that large rock over there?"

She nodded, her breath catching. Had it been her imagination, or had he been about to kiss her? Under normal circumstances, that would have seemed insane.

Yet, somehow—in that singular moment—nothing could have felt more right.

Sam secured an arm around his waist and hobbled along as Jake supported her. She was overwrought and not thinking clearly. Reading too much into the situation. Perhaps if she'd heeded her friends' advice and rejoined the dating scene after leaving Nelson, she wouldn't be having such absurd notions concerning a stranger she'd met along a Virginia road.

They reached the boulder and he gingerly released her, making sure she kept her balance. "Hang on just a sec," he said, before tugging off his extra sweater, sliding it past broad shoulders. The motion caused the lower layer of his clothing to rise, briefly exposing his taut six pack. Muscles rippled then quickly disappeared as he shook out the sweater and laid it on the boulder. "Now that we've gotten you dry..." He shot her a wink. "Let's keep it that way."

Sam swallowed hard, her tailbone tingling. "Won't you be cold?"

"I'm warming up," he said with a grin. "How about you?"

Sam tried to speak intelligently but all she could offer was, "Um-hum." Her mind was still lost in that tantalizing glimpse of flesh and the feel of being in his arms. She wasn't supposed to be thinking these thoughts, not here and now, but it was almost like she couldn't help it. Jake had her under some sort of spell and his magic was irresistible.

He eased her onto the boulder, then carefully slipped off her loafer, testing the bones of her ankle with his fingers. "How does that feel?"

"Not too sore to the touch," she admitted. "It mostly hurts when I stand."

He nodded and grasped her toes through her sock, gingerly pressing them back and forth. One iteration was too much. "Ow!" A shock of pain shot up her ankle to her calf.

He rested the heel of her foot in his hand. "I don't think it's sprained. You probably strained a ligament."

Sam felt her forehead crease. "I'm not staying here."

Jake laughed out loud at the unexpected comment. "Nobody asked you to." He gently slid her loafer back on. "You should get along just fine. Might slow you down a smidge, but I'll be here to help you. We can take our time. Miss Beulah's can't be that far away now."

"Miss Beulah's? But I thought we were looking for the diner?"

"How about we go for whatever we come to first?" He gave her a dashing smile, moonlight offsetting the lines of his face. "Like whatever's making that glow over there?"

Sam startled, seeing the fog had completely lifted. Through the mountain pass, a light glimmered in the distance.

"You think it's a house?"

"One way to find out!" He helped her stand, ushering her along.

She glanced at him sideways. "You're suddenly optimistic."

"That's because there's more good news." He held his free hand out beside him, palm up. "The sky's stopped spitting. Looks like I might not be needing that slicker after all."

"But your keys?"

"If that's a house up there"—he gestured with his chin—"the owner's sure to know about Becky's. Might possibly give us a ride back there to pick up the slicker. *After* we've called for help and are sure roadside assistance is on its way.

"Failing that, we'll just ask the tow truck to make a pit stop on the way back to my SUV. Dropping by the diner shouldn't take us that far off course."

Sam looked at him and grinned. "You've got this all figured out, haven't you?"

"Yes, ma'am," he said with assurance. But the truth was, inside himself, Jake didn't have this figured out well at all. What had he been thinking when he'd taken Sam in his arms? Had he actually been drawn to her lips? Was he crazy enough to want to kiss her? Jake was a firm believer that there's a time and place for everything, and this clearly wasn't the place or situation in which to think of something like romance. Sam wasn't interested. She was *injured.* And that had happened on his watch.

He was grateful this injury was minor, and one that would likely resolve itself. The ankle might smart for a bit, but she'd be able to tolerate more pressure as time went on. She was moving well enough now; he doubted she'd even need it splinted. "How's the ankle doing?"

"Better." She gave him a weak smile as she inched forward. She was tucked under his arm and grabbing on to his waist as he helped her along. It was a little awkward walking this way, but the truth was that Jake didn't mind it. He hadn't been this close to a female in a long time. Though he regretted the circumstances, having Sam snuggled up beside him actually felt good. It was almost like she belonged there. In fact, it made him a little sad when she pulled away.

Jake watched as Sam shifted her balance from her good foot to her weakened side, then back again. "I think I can walk on my own now," she said, looking up.

"Are you sure?"

"We'll make better time if I'm moving under my own steam," she stated reasonably.

But when she met his eyes all reason flew out the window and all he could think of was taking her in his arms again. How long had it been since he'd felt that way about a woman? Only one word came to mind: *forever.* Jake's heart pounded and his lips felt dry. There was only one way to quench them. Sam's mouth was an oasis, and he'd been without water too long. He could get lost in her and he knew it. *Lost, body and soul.*

Her brow arched with concern. "Are you okay?"

Jake's throat constricted. Here he was the one who was supposed to be under control, and he'd nearly lost it. All over one compelling woman with gorgeous blue eyes.

"Yep—" He coughed into his hand when his voice broke apart like a teenager's. "Fine." His chest was still burning, but at this point it was hard to tell whether it was from the aftereffects of the smoke or merely thinking of Sam. Jake was normally a rational guy, but something about her undid him.

Sam turned to face him. "I want to thank you. For everything you've done...and are doing...for me."

He tried to make light of the moment and ignore the fact that his heart was still racing. "I'm doing it for the two of us."

"I know you have some place to be too." She smiled softly. "I'm glad that neither of us is stuck out here alone."

"There's safety in numbers."

His dark eyes sparkled and Sam wondered if that
was true. Safety in three or more, for sure. But how safe
was she when it was just the two of them? Not that Sam
worried about Jake being any sort of physical danger to
her. Just think of all he'd done to help her—including
that daring rescue from her burning car. If Jake were
the sort of man with bad motives, he clearly would have
acted on those already. But Jake didn't seem the bad
sort at all. In fact, he appeared just the opposite. Like
the kind of guy who took his responsibilities seriously,
and deeply cared for people. Which left Sam wondering
if Jake had a girlfriend or a wife. She judged him to be
in his early thirties, so somewhere along the line he
must have had the opportunity. He certainly had a
powerful magnetism. She'd felt it the moment she'd
been wrapped in his arms, which was just one more
reason she'd needed to pull away. What if Jake *was*
involved with someone? She certainly had no business
tempting fate while they were thrown together,
particularly as this situation was only temporary.

"Ah yes," she answered. "Two heads are also
better than one." She gestured down the road. "Which
is why we ought to put our heads together and find out
what's over there."

Sam couldn't help but think of her father, and her
primary mission of getting home. While Sam had
prepared herself for the worst during the course of his
illness, the severity of the situation hadn't sunk in until
she'd begun her trek across the mountains. She'd had
the best dad ever, who'd always been there for her.
Now, she needed to stay strong for him. Her fortitude
during any transition would be a boon to her mom, and

that was the very best way to honor her Papa. It's what he would want.

"Sam?" Jake's voice called through the mist. She turned to find him staring at her.

Sam stealthily lifted a hand to wipe back a tear she hoped Jake hadn't seen. "I'm sorry. Did you say something?"

He studied her with compassion. "I said, you're right. Let's go."

Jake held out his hand and Sam took it, feeling—in an inexplicable sense—she'd go anywhere with this man. Then he wrapped his fingers around hers, and led her toward the light.

Chapter Ten

Wind howled through the dark tunnel ahead, echoing off rocky mountain walls. Each rose more than forty feet, towering toward a coal-black sky and ending in icy peaks. Beyond those, stars studded the night, twinkling in and out of cloud cover. The moon wasn't visible now, having been blocked, Jake supposed, by a looming mountain ridge. He was grateful he had his flashlight illuminating the path before them. But the moment he had that thought, its light flickered, then dimmed. Sam tightened her grasp on his hand. "Jake," she whispered, "I have a funny feeling—"

The wind picked up, drowning out her words and moaning like a tortured old woman.

Jake braced himself against the tingles racing down his spine.

"It's all ri—" he started, before the wind ripped past again, blasting them from either side. Sam shrieked and leapt toward Jake. He tugged her against him with one arm, while panning the area with the faint beam of the light in his other hand.

Wild gusts sent Sam's hair streaming across her face. She turned her head, pressing her cheek to Jake's chest. Jake's pulse pounded in his ears and his heart beat like a kettledrum.

Then, the flashlight blinked twice and went out.

Sam wound her other arm around him, and the ineffective flashlight crashed to the ground. It clanked against the road and burst open, its face dislodging as two cylinders rolled onto the asphalt. He was surprised the batteries had lasted this long. It was foolish to hope he could put things back together and press them into further service.

Sam's chin trembled. "Jake…"

He cupped her head to his chest and made a soothing sound, stroking her hair. "It's just the wind."

She whimpered as it roared again.

"I'm not going to let anything happen to you." He tightened his arms around her. "Hey…"

She looked up.

"We're going to get through this. We're going to find help."

His expression was tender and sure. If Jake believed it, then she should too. What reason did she have to doubt him? Her eyes snagged on the shattered flashlight on the road. "We've lost our one source of light."

"Then we'll follow that one." He nodded toward the end of the mountain pass. Beyond the narrow opening, there was a hint of broader terrain—and the bright, encouraging glimmer they'd seen earlier. He lowered his face to hers. "Are you with me?"

Either the wind had abated, or Sam had become lost in the heat of Jake's stare. His warm perusal poured over her, causing a deep thaw in her bones. It was impossible to feel chilled when she was in Jake's arms. He'd vowed to protect her and Sam trusted he would.

But who would look after Jake? Sam determined to pull herself together, understanding that she alone could be that person. No one else was here to do the job. If a situation arose where Jake needed her, she'd have to step forward—just as he had for her.

"Yes," she told him surely. She slid her palms down his arms, then took both his hands in hers. "I'm here for you too," she said, holding them firmly.

He gave her a lazy grin. "It's good to know a beautiful woman has my back."

Sam's cheeks fired at the compliment. Now, she was nowhere near cold. She was boiling. "You've probably had lots of experience with that."

"Not really."

"That's hard to believe."

He held her gaze a fraction of a second longer, something telling in his eyes. "You can believe it or not, but I'm somewhat of a loner."

Sam thought of the solitary life she led. "So am I."

His lips pulled into a grin. "Now *that's* a hard one to believe."

Sam fell into Jake's eyes and time stopped moving. All at once it was like the rest of the world had gone away and it was just the two of them. Sam wondered what it would be like having a relationship with Jake. She'd worried earlier that he might be involved with someone else, but he'd indicated that he was single, and Sam had just hinted at her availability too.

These same raging thoughts must have been tearing through Jake's brain, because his ears were tinged red and his eyes burned hot with desire. He took a step toward her, then appeared to rein himself in. This clearly wasn't the place or the time; he must have been telling himself that too. Though Sam wondered if he really believed it.

Jake released one of her hands, still grasping the other. "Let's get going," he said with a tug. "There are things we can discuss later that are better said indoors."

Sam's hopeful heart read between the lines. Was he indicating that he too thought they might have some kind of future, once this awful mess got sorted out? Sam's primary goal was getting to her father. But her Papa had her Mama, and always had. For as long as Sam could remember, her parents had shared a loving partnership. She'd nearly given up on finding that kind of relationship for herself. The experience with Nelson had left her with a bitter taste in her mouth, and she hadn't met anyone to sweeten her expectations since.

Sam tightened her hold on Jake's hand, sensing something had changed between them. They'd shared intimacies. Their relationship had deepened. They weren't exactly friends, but they were no longer total strangers. In her heart, Sam wondered if they could be lovers. Though she understood Jake was right: They'd have to save that conversation for another day. At the moment, all that mattered was getting to River Falls.

As they made for the pass, Sam stopped and turned back toward the boulder. "Your sweater!" she cried, remembering they'd left it behind.

He gave her hand a squeeze. "Don't need it anymore."

"But we can't just—"

"We'll come back for it later, all right? Right now, we've got to see what's over there."

Chapter Eleven

When they finally reached the clearing at the other side of the pass, the sky opened up above them. The moon was hidden by the clouds, making way for a luminous star to light up the night. Its glow streamed into the valley below, cascading in shimmers into a glistening pond.

"That's what made the light seem so bright," Jake said. "Its reflection on the water."

Not just on the water, Sam thought, her eyes scanning the side of a nearby mountain. It hung heavy with dripping icicles, also catching the bright star's sheen. The pointy downward spikes sparkled magically, giving Sam the sense she was in a distant realm. She viewed the star with wonder, catching her breath on the word. "Polaris."

"The North Star," Jake affirmed.

"It can help us find our way home."

Jake met Sam's eyes.

"Papa... I mean, my father, he explained..." She shook her head, remembering. "Of course he would. He was—he *is*— a scientist—"

"Scientist?" Jake questioned.

"Astronomer, really." She set her chin at the fond memory. "He was always taking me out to see the stars."

"Your father...?" Jake's eyes lit with understanding, as if he'd put something together. "Your dad is Ben Williams? *You're* Samantha...Williams?"

She released his hand with a gasp. "Yes, but how did you—?"

"Sam..." He studied her seriously. "The client I'm going to River Falls to see? It's your dad."

"What?"

"He's come across a big invention, something involving a major telescope and its lens. Something that might expand our reach into other galaxies by a magnitude of ten thousand. It could absolutely change the course of astronomy."

"I knew he was working on a secret project. He's labored on it for years. He never told us what it was about."

"He's not quite done with his trials," Jake told her. "But he's close enough to believe he'll have success. He wanted to protect his invention for the use of future astronomers, and he hoped to secure any potential monetary benefit for his family."

"It's hard to see how a find like that could be of—"

"His super lens technology could have other applications. Be used in certain forms of surgery. Maybe even in the IT field. Your dad is a highly intelligent man, and smart enough to know he may be sitting on a gold mine."

"I had no idea." Sam's first reaction was extreme pride, but then her heart sank. Her dad had spent years on this project, and now he might not be here to see it to fruition. And in the midst of it all, he'd thought of them: her and her mother.

Jake steadied her shoulders in his hands. "I'm telling you this because I want you to know how much your dad cares. How much he's thought of you and your mom."

Even without this latest development, Sam would have known that, yet she appreciated Jake filling her in. "What about your law firm's stand on confidentiality?"

"My boss is your father's long-term friend. They go way back to high school. When he sent me on this trip, he instructed me to communicate the particulars of the situation to Ben's family, just in case—"

Sam's chin quivered. "My dad didn't make it."

"No. In case he was in a position where he couldn't communicate."

"He was conscious when I talked to Mama."

"Yes, but going in for triple-bypass surgery. I was trying to get there before that."

"Me too." Sam hung her head. "The doctors couldn't offer any guarantees. With one surgery—okay. But this is his second operation in less than two years. My dad was on medication, but—"

Jake righted her chin in his hand. "There's still a chance he'll pull through this."

"A slim one."

Sam searched Jake's eyes. "I really wanted to be there," she said, her voice cracking. "I don't even know at this point if he's…"

Her voice fell off in a wavering whisper and Jake pulled her to him.

"That's why you seemed so familiar. Your gestures, your demeanor, and in particular those bright blue eyes… They're just like your dad's."

Jake had met Ben Williams a couple of times when he'd come into the office for consultations. His boss had brought him in on the case because he was a big believer in having backup. In this instance that had been a good idea, as his boss had been unable to make this last-minute trip himself. They'd been drawing up the paperwork for the patent application and getting Ben's new estate papers in order when they'd received the call that Ben had been rushed to the hospital and another operation was imminent. Apparently, the last thing he'd said to his wife Lisa before being lifted into the ambulance was, "Get Jake Marlow here."

Sam sobbed against his shoulder. "I have to get home."

"I know." He stroked her hair and held her close. "And, I'm going to take you there. I promise you that. If it's the last thing I do."

Then he hugged her more tightly and let her cry…until her tears were all cried out.

Chapter Twelve

Jake cradled Sam in his arms until the height of her anguish passed and she stopped weeping. Of course she was beside herself. Jake would be too, were he in a similar circumstance. Just like Sam, Jake had been lucky enough to have a good father. Great parents in fact. Both were still doing well in the new home they'd set up for their early retirement to Santa Fe. His dad was a retired builder and his mom a self-employed painter. She'd already been commissioned to paint several murals in New Mexico, and didn't plan to pack away her paintbrushes any time soon. Perhaps this partially explained why Jake felt such a soft spot for Sam. She had artistic leanings like his mom and, from the evidence he'd seen, Sam also possessed enormous talent. Though he didn't know Sam well, it was still wrenching to see her so heartbroken over her father. He wished to goodness his prognosis of Sam's dad's recovery would come true. But, as Sam said, the doctors hadn't offered any guarantees.

"My mom's an artist, you know," he whispered to the head resting against his shoulder.

Sam sniffed, but didn't look up. "Is she really? What kind?"

"Oil painter. But she does murals too. She's working on a couple now, in fact."

Sam pulled back to look at him, but her eyes still brimmed with sadness. "You're being very kind. Thinking of other things to say. To take my mind off—"

"No, it's not that." He grinned. "Though I'm glad to hear you think of me as kind.
The truth is, I just now thought of it—the comparison between you and my mom. Perhaps that's why I like you so much."

Did he imagine it, or did her cheeks turn pink?

"Do you?" Sam dragged her palms across her cheeks, drying them. "Even considering the mess that I am?"

His dark eyes caught the starlight. "You're a gorgeous mess from where I stand."

"And you're one horrible flirt!"

"Horrible? Really?" He forced a play pout. "I was hoping I was pretty good at it."

In spite of herself, Sam smiled. "You really do have a way with words, sometimes."

"A good way, I'd suppose?"

"Yes. Excellent."

"That's great to hear. I was starting to fear for my ego."

"It's that fragile, is it?"

"Like a crystal vase."

Sam sputtered a laugh. The last thing she could imagine this strong guy being was delicate.

"It's true." He met her eyes and his gaze lingered. "I may look tough on the outside, but right in here..." He splayed the fingers of his right hand against his chest. "Lies a very tender heart."

"I'll try to remember that."

Time froze as they stood there in the starlight, neither one daring to move. Sam couldn't believe how attracted to him she was. Though it was understandable, of course. Here was this man who'd appeared from out of nowhere to help her and champion her cause in getting home. Sam understood now that she'd been destined to meet Jake one way or another. They lived in the same town and he'd been bound for River Falls, just as she was, the two of them rushing to the aid of her dad—only Mother Nature had thrown her a curveball by forcing her off the road. Then, mysteriously, the fates had come to her rescue, delivering a handsome hero just in time. Sam shuddered to think of what might have happened to her if Jake hadn't arrived precisely when he did. But he had, and he was here now, vowing to keep her safe.

"You know what they say about the North Star?" he asked her.

Sam slowly shook her head.

"It never falters. Never changes."

"It's a constant."

"In a constant world of change."

"You think it can get us home?"

"I believe it can lead us to Miss Beulah's."

"How's that?"

"Remember when Becky said Miss Beulah's place was just east of the diner?"

"Yeah?"

"Well, she didn't send us east. She sent us west."

"Why would she do that?"

"I'm sure she didn't mean to. She was facing us when she gave us directions. Her back was to the kitchen. She was probably used to taking that turn when the diner was ahead of her. She motioned for us to turn right, which meant we should have gone left. We were seeing a mirror image. Things were flipped around."

In a crazy way, Jake was making sense. But they'd covered so much ground already and hadn't seen any signs of a house.

Jake spoke as if knowing her thoughts. "We haven't gone as far as you think. We covered most of our territory heading in the wrong direction. We probably missed the turn to the diner just like you said. It was lost in the fog."

"Even so. Surely we've gone more than a mile by now."

Jake glanced over her shoulder with a smile. "It would seem so."

Sam turned to see what had caught his eye and her heart stilled. She could scarcely believe it, but there it was! Not a hundred yards ahead of them sat a house, still partially shrouded by the fog that was lifting off the road. A light burned in one of its windows. "Jake!"

"I know." He reached out and took her hand. "How's that ankle holding up?"

She shifted her weight and put more pressure on it. It ached a little, but was serviceable. "It's fine to walk. Truth is, I could almost run!"

Jake tugged at her hand, holding her back. "Whoa," he said. "No need to rush this part and risk hurting yourself further. We're almost there."

Chapter Thirteen

Lisa put another candle in the window. She always kept one burning for Jimmy, and now she added a second one for Sam. Perhaps she was superstitious to believe it would help, but she was crazy with worry. The last she'd heard from her daughter, Sam had been on the way and approaching the highway. She should have made River Falls hours ago. At first, Lisa blamed it on a weather delay. Then she'd been preoccupied at the hospital. The surgery had been interminable, each minute ticking by slowly as her pulse drummed in her ears, drowning out the waiting room television and the coffeepot dripping in the lounge nearby. Finally, it was done and Ben had survived it. Whether or not he'd survive the recovery was another story. Lisa was loath to leave the hospital, but its staff had encouraged her to go home and rest for just a little while. He would be in recovery for several hours before getting moved to the Cardiac Intensive Care Unit, so she might as well take a breather while she could. Like Lisa could even think of breathing without him. Ben was her whole life, her destiny. They'd met during their third year of college and had been inseparable ever since.

No other man had ever interested her, and Ben wasn't the sort to have a roving eye. He'd been a caring and loyal husband, and the world's best dad. Lisa choked back a sob, drawing a tissue to her mouth. She couldn't bear to lose him, and now her heart pounded with fear concerning Sam. She'd been so sure Sam would show up at the hospital to surprise her in the family waiting room with a hug. Sam had always been a good child and a gracious daughter, but she'd been her daddy's girl. Just like Jimmy had been his Mama's boy. Lisa buried her face in her hands, the brutal irony tearing through her. She'd already lost Jimmy, and now Ben's life hung in the balance. If something were to happen to Sam as well...

Sobs racked her body as Lisa doubled forward clutching her arms to her chest. When Sam hadn't appeared at the hospital, Lisa had convinced herself that Sam had probably tried to call. She'd been hung up somewhere, and had a logical explanation. But when Lisa got beyond the zone of the hospital that blocked cellular calls, she saw that no incoming messages had registered on her phone. The only thing Lisa could think of was that perhaps Sam had driven straight home. When Lisa left the hospital, it wasn't to *take a breather,* it was to look for Sam. But when she'd returned here, Sam's car wasn't in the drive. What's more, nothing in the house looked disturbed. She'd even checked Sam's bedroom, just in case she'd dropped off her luggage and hurried to the hospital. It wasn't likely Sam and Lisa would have missed each other passing on the two-lane road that ran into town, but it was possible. *No. It wasn't.*

Lisa fought back her panic as she reached for the phone.

There was only one thing left for her to do.
Call the highway patrol.

Sam and Jake approached the cozy cabin that sat at
the edge of the woods. It appeared to be a simple log
construction with an old tin roof. Cheery light emanated
from a window beside the front door. As they drew
closer, Sam saw the light streamed from a large ginger
jar lamp inside. It wasn't a plastic Christmas candle like
her mom typically left on at home. Jimmy had gone
missing during the Christmas season. When the
holidays ended, Lisa had removed all the candles from
the windows and packed them away. All of them but
one. Even after Jimmy had been declared officially lost
at sea, she'd refused to remove it, proclaiming she'd
leave it in place until she finally had his body to lay to
rest. Jimmy's untimely death had been heart-wrenching
for the entire family, but Sam understood there was
something extra poignant about a mother's grief.
Particularly as Jimmy and her mom had been so close.

Sam thought she spied movement indoors beyond
the lampshade, a figure in a military uniform. She drew
her hand to her mouth. *"Jimmy."*

Jake tightened his hold on her other hand and
stared in the window. "Did you see someone?"

"I…" Sam's eyes had to be playing tricks on her,
given the lateness of the hour, the trials of the day, and
the fact that she'd just been thinking of her brother.
"I'm not sure."

"Probably Miss Beulah," Jake said. He released her
hand and searched for a doorbell. Not finding one, he
rapped on the heavy wood door. The sound of his
knocking echoed…one…two…three times.

Sam expected to hear footsteps approaching from the inside, but there were none.

Jake tilted his head to peer through the window. "It's almost like someone's expecting us. There's a fire burning in the hearth."

Sam drew up beside him to peek through the murky glass. The room appeared homespun and cheery. A plaid love seat faced the window and overstuffed armchairs perched by the hearth, its embers burning low. A neat stack of logs sat beside it, and it looked as if one of them had been recently added to the fire. Flames leapt, casting shadows across the worn hook rug, whose colors picked up the tones of the ginger jar lamps arranged around the room. Before the sofa, a handsomely hewn oak coffee table held an assortment of oddly shaped books and piles of loose photographs.

"Either that, or Miss Beulah's a night owl," replied Sam.

Jake rapped at the door again, but got no answer.

"How odd," Sam said. "Someone's clearly home."

She raised a hand to knock herself, but the second her knuckles made contact with the door—it creaked open.

Chapter Fourteen

The door swung wide and a rush of heat raced toward them. Sam fell back against Jake's chest, shielding her face with her arms at the blast.

Jake steadied her shoulders in his hands and stared beyond her into the empty room. It was warm all right, particularly when compared to the chill of the night air. "Toasty."

And bright. Sam squinted against the assault of light. She'd become so accustomed to the darkness, her eyes had trouble adjusting. "Hello!" Sam stepped into the house and Jake followed. "Anybody home?"

Jake called louder, "Miss Beulah?"

But the only reply was the soft crackling of logs in the fireplace.

"A little weird," Jake whispered.

Sam whispered back, "More than a little."

Jake surveyed the flight of steps. "Maybe she's up—" His words fell off when he saw Sam staring at the coffee table.

She'd noticed books strewn on it while peering through the window. Now that she drew closer, she discerned that one of them was a yearbook. *Wait a minute.* Sam snatched it up, her heart hammering.

"Sam? What is—?"

"This can't be," she said hoarsely. "Can't be right." She glanced at Jake, then flipped the book open and rapidly scanned through its pages. When she came to her class year, she stopped. "It's mine," she told Jake, looking up.

"What do you mean it's yours?"

She partially closed the book, revealing the cover. It showcased a handsome brick building, Blue Ridge High. "This is where I went to school."

"Then it's a coincidence," Jake said. "Miss Beulah's daughter—the doctor—maybe she...or another one of Miss Beulah's kids..."

Sam was still flipping through the pages, scarcely hearing a word he said. Then she landed on her picture. "Oh my, I'd nearly forgotten."

"Forgotten what?"

"How young I was."

"You were just a kid, right? Had to have been eight or nine years ago."

"Ten."

Jake studied the rectangular color photo. The seniors apparently had been granted larger, more glamorous pictures than the others in the book. "One thing hasn't changed."

Sam met his eyes as he said, "You were a looker then too."

Normally, Sam might have blushed, but she was way beyond being flirted with now. Something was happening here. Something bizarre.

Jake surveyed her kindly. "Don't read too much into it. Okay? It's just a book."

"Yeah? Then what are all of those?" Sam grabbed a stack of photos from the coffee table, sorting through them. All at once, her head felt light and her stomach went sour.

Jake laid a hand on her arm. "Sam?"

Her voice wavered. "I…I think I need to sit down." She backed against the love seat, her knees shaking, then plunked down onto a cushion, photos dumped in her lap. Jake sat beside her and picked up a small square photograph resting on Sam's knee. It was a black-and-white photo of a couple standing with a young boy. The woman was holding a baby.

Sam's voice came out flat, with no intonation in it at all. "That's me."

Jake choked out his reply. "What? Sam, that's craz—"

She shoved another photo under his nose and Jake stopped short. It was a picture of a little girl with long golden braids. She grinned broadly at the camera, her two front teeth missing. But the smile was unmistakable. Jake's heart thudded. "That's you as a child?"

Sam nodded numbly, and handed him another photo. "And me, in middle school." Jake stared in shock at the girl on the new ten-speed bike.

She shared a photo of her looking a little older and all dressed up with a guy in a tux. "Me, with my first boyfriend at my high-school prom."

Perspiration beaded Jake's brow. He was getting overheated in his sweater. Either that, or he was sitting too close to the fire. "I don't get it. What is this?"

Sam looked up and met his eyes, fear and acknowledgment in hers. "My life."

Lisa tore into the emergency room, her heart racing. "My daughter!" she cried, grabbing the lapels of the first person she came to. "They said she was brought in here!"

The kindly EMT with a name tag that read "Darryl" rested his bag on the floor. "Becky!" he shouted at the female EMT heading through the sliding door and toward an open ambulance.

She turned, her eyes registering understanding the moment she saw Lisa.

Becky called into the ambulance. "Be just a minute, Leroy." Then she strode briskly in Lisa's direction, the furrows deepening in her brow as she approached.

Chapter Fifteen

Sam set aside the photographs with trembling fingers. "Jake," she said, "I think something happened in my car. Something we didn't understand."

He took her hand. "Don't be ridiculous. I got you out of there. I got *us* out of there. Remember?"

Sam shook her head, then caught movement at the top of the stairs. A military uniform. U.S. Navy. She sprang to her feet. *"Jimmy!"* The name sliced from her throat, tearing like a jagged saw. Jake tried to hold her back, but she broke away from his grasp, racing for the stairs.

"Sam, no!" Jake caught her from behind and wrapped his arms around her. She struggled in his hold.

"Let me go!"

"I can't. I won't." His breath was labored.

She wiggled fiercely, digging her elbows into his gut. He groaned, but held her tighter. "Sam!" he cautioned. "You've got to calm down, you've got to—"

She wrenched herself free of his arms, spinning to face him. "Calm down, Jake? *Calm down?*"

He held out his hands, palms out. "Easy…"

Jake inched toward her and Sam stepped back.

"Sam," he told her, "you can do this. You and I can do this. I promised you. I *swore* I'd keep you—"

He was not quite within reach of her.

Seizing the opportunity, she turned and bolted up the stairs.

"What's happened to my daughter?" Lisa asked the lady EMT.

Becky motioned for Lisa to sit on one of the waiting room's plastic-lined sofas. Lisa was beside herself with worry, her head whirling at a nauseating tilt.

Becky's voice was low and gentle, but still held a southern twang. "You're speaking of Samantha, right?"

Lisa thought she nodded, but couldn't feel the bob of her chin. It was like her whole face had gone numb. "Samantha Williams, that's right." The inside of her mouth felt like plaster of Paris, all clogged and sticky.

Becky's gray eyes creased at the corners and they seemed a little damp, almost like she'd been crying herself. "You'll need to talk to the lady in admitting," she said softly. "Tell her who you are, that you're family."

"Admitting?" Lisa grasped at the thread. Of course, Sam had been admitted. When the highway patrol had finally called back, that's what they'd said. And if she'd been admitted, then she had to be… "She's fine then?" Lisa pressed. "My little girl's going to be all right?"

"Sam!" Jake called, tearing after her. "Don't!"

But it was too late, she'd already rushed ahead, taking the steps two at a time, then pivoting on the landing. She thought she'd seen her brother go that way, down the hall. "Jimmy!" she cried. The fear coursing through her veins was overcome by the joy in her heart. It was him. It had to be. After all this time.

Sam ran into a back bedroom, then paused, finding it empty. Her head reeled with confusion as her eyes panned across the recesses of the narrow space. It was a small room, not much different from a navy bunker. From somewhere far away, music played, maybe from a radio. A crackling radio, with poor reception like the old-fashioned kind.

Sam scanned the small space again, searching out the source of the sound. It seemed to be coming from overhead.

That's when she saw it. A long, thin cord, dangling from a pull-down door in the ceiling, the sort that led up to an attic. Around the perimeters of the door, something shone through from the other side. A piercingly bright light.

Chapter Sixteen

Becky folded her hands together and rested them in her lap. She had short brown hair and a caring face that had been weathered by time. "I'm afraid I can't give you any information on your daughter's current condition." Her hands clasped each other. "You'll have to ask to speak with the admitting physician."

"But you know about her?" Lisa pressed. "You were in the ambulance that picked her up?"

Becky didn't avert her gaze. "Yes, ma'am."

"And…" Lisa drew a breath. "How was she? When you found her?"

"I'm not supposed to—"

"Please," Lisa pleaded. "I'm her mother. You were there."

Becky momentarily hung her head. "Cold. Wet." When she looked up, her voice cracked. "In bad shape."

Lisa's heart caught in her throat. "Define bad shape," she forced herself to say.

"She'd broken some ribs, ma'am, and likely punctured a lung. We gave her oxygen, wrapped her in blankets to bring up her body temperature…" Becky stopped talking. It was obvious she was trying to pull herself together and remain professional. "Hooked her up to an IV, tried to stabilize her on the way into town, but there was nothing we could do for..." Becky turned away.

Lisa gripped Becky's forearm with her right hand.

Becky met Lisa's eyes. "I'm no specialist."

"But you suspected something."

"She'd hit her head pretty hard. Was unconscious. There could have been swelling in the—"

Before she got to the word *brain,* Lisa pushed herself off the sofa. "Thank you." She quickly shook the EMT's hand while her own trembled. "Thanks for taking care of her, and bringing her here."

Then she hurried toward the admissions desk to learn where Sam was now.

Sam reached for the cord and yanked down the door, seconds before Jake entered the room. Stairs cascaded open before her, spilling out like an accordion. Sam locked the ladder in place and set her foot on its first rung. She reached higher with her hands, preparing to climb.

"Sam." She glanced over her shoulder to find Jake walking toward her.

"Don't try to stop me!" Sam wheezed, suddenly aware she was nearly out of breath. The stitch in her side had returned with a vengeance. She released the ladder with one hand to clutch her ribcage.

"I've never been here to stop you." His expression was calm, a sweet serenity in his dark-brown eyes. "I've only wanted to help."

He walked toward her, but this time Sam stayed in place. It was like she knew she could take him at his word. Jake didn't mean to harm her, he never had. He brushed a hand to her cheek and Sam's heart stilled.

"Everything's going to be okay now. You're going home."

"Me? What about you?"

A lazy smile tilted up one edge of his mouth. "We'll meet again."

What? *No.* "You...you can't mean you brought me all this way just to—?"

"Sam," he said, stopping her. "They're waiting for you. It's best to move along."

Without warning or forethought, Sam found herself leaping into his arms. "You're coming with me." Tears blurred her vision and her voice grew shaky. She hugged him harder. "You have to!"

He hugged her to him, nesting her cheek against his chest and resting his chin on the top of her head. His voice was husky when he spoke. "You know, I'd like that very much."

The noise above them grew louder. People talking. And music. But the strangest music Sam had ever heard. Yet she found herself entranced by it, like it was urging her on. Sam glanced up the ladder, then back into Jake's eyes. They were incredible eyes, dark and soulful. "Let's go," she told him. "Before it's too late."

Jake nodded and helped her get her footing on the ladder. "Ladies first."

His breath was a light tickle at the side of her neck. Sam felt herself shiver and grow warm all over. The light pouring down on her was blinding, like a spotlight, but she was still driven to go toward it. Jake's arms cradled hers on the handrails, as he offered stalwart support from behind. "Keep going," he encouraged.

She had every intention to, but Sam had to do something important first.

She turned partially to face him and slipped an arm around his neck.

His eyebrows rose, questioning. "Sam?"

She didn't think she'd ever find the proper words to thank him. If it hadn't been for Jake, she wouldn't be here now. He'd cared for her and protected her. He'd listened to her stories and shared tales of his own. Nothing had ever felt this right.

When she'd fallen into his arms, it was like she was meant to stay there. And when he'd held her in the starlight, it was like he understood. Like he sensed the pain she was going through and only wanted to soothe it. Now she had to show him just how much that meant, and exactly how she felt. For somehow this seemed fuzzy, as if she were in a dream... If she didn't act soon, she risked waking up—without Jake knowing.

Oh, how she wanted to lay her mouth on his and become lost in his sweetness forever, because, somehow, *forever* was written in his eyes. "I need to kiss you," she said, believing that completely.

He stepped up on the ladder, bringing his body flush with hers, and pulled her to him. His lips were merely a hairbreadth away when he spoke with a throaty whisper. "Are you sure?"

Sam had never been more committed to anything in her life.

She must have nodded without realizing, because the next thing she knew, his mouth was on hers, consuming it with a hungry passion. Heat welled in her cheeks and fire filled her veins as he kissed her deeply, steadying her against the ladder. One hand cradled her head, his fingers threading through her hair, while the other reached high to a rung, pinning them in place in a heated embrace. Jake's rock-solid frame pressed into hers and Sam heard herself whimper when she felt his response.

Her world flashed with bright lights, at first in black and white, and then in rainbow colors.

"Jake," she breathed, as he kissed her again, varying the pressure of his lips, teasing her and tasting her. Or was it she who had taken the lead? Sam no longer cared who was in charge, just as long as this didn't end. Her pulse picked up and her blood pumped harder. She was a furnace at her very core. It was an entirely new sensation, consuming in its power. And that power came on like a steam engine...roaring forward with full force. If there was a ladder at her back she didn't feel it. Perhaps it had melted away. Into a field of daylilies, sweet and fragrant, swaying gently in the breeze—just as light as Jake's softening kisses.

He gave her one last satiny brush of his lips and whispered, "It's time to go."

Sam opened her eyes, her head spinning...her heart beating wildly. She could barely catch her breath.

Then, she heard her brother's voice.

"Not yet."

Sam stared over Jake's shoulder. "Jimmy!" She'd been so scared that she'd lost him, or had imagined... He studied her fondly.

"It's going to be all right now."

The thought hit her with a jolt. She and Jake were going home. They couldn't leave Jimmy behind. "You have to come with us!" she said, reaching past Jake and toward him. She tried to descend the ladder but Jake blocked her with his broad frame.

"Jake?" she pleaded staring up at him.

Jake glanced at Jimmy, who set his chin. "You're halfway there," Jimmy told her, "you have to keep moving."

Her voice rang out in panic. "But I can't! You have to come too!"

Jimmy eyed the attic door opening, then signaled to Jake to herd his sister along. Jake gave Sam a small nudge up the ladder, and uncertainty burned through her. The light...it was tugging...like a magnet. And the voices... They were calling her. *But I can't go without Jimmy.* She turned back to her brother, who trapped her in his gaze. It was calm and reassuring, like time was of no consequence. Why then did Sam feel her seconds ticking away?

"I want you to do something for me," Jimmy said. "I want you to tell Mama I'm okay."

Sam was about to protest further when a hand reached through the gaping hole above and grabbed her wrist.

Chapter Seventeen

Lisa stood by the admitting desk feeling like her legs were dredged in quicksand. The receptionist checking the records was taking eons to go through her computer files.

The heavyset middle-aged woman looked up from her clicking mouse. She had a humorless face. Not that Lisa felt anything like humor at the moment. In fact, she was sick to her stomach. "You might want to have a seat."

Lisa did as she was told, worrying that this would mean further delays. How long could it take to pull up one name? "It's Williams," she reinforced. "Samantha Williams. W-I-L-L—"

The receptionist looked up. "I know how to spell Williams, ma'am." She adjusted the square glasses frames on the bridge of her nose. "I'm just clearing up the fact that there are two of them in the system."

Lisa's heart sank. She'd been in such a stew over Sam, she'd neglected to think of Ben, or how his recovery was going. "Yes, the other one—Benjamin—he's my husband."

The woman observed her with interest. It wasn't quite compassion. "You've had quite a day."

"Exactly." Lisa felt as though she were wasting her breath. She glanced toward the circular drive that led to the emergency room, seeing Becky's ambulance had gone. "Ben came out of surgery earlier this evening. Was waiting to get transferred to the CICU."

"Dr. Hampton's been trying to reach you."

"What?" Lisa checked her purse, finding her cell phone missing. She must have left it charging on the kitchen counter. When she'd received the call from the state police, she'd been in such a rush—

"I said, Dr. Hampton's been trying to reach you about your husband."

Fear gripped Lisa's gut. "What's happened? Is something wrong?"

"You'll have to speak to the doctor yourself."

"Is he in the hospital?"

"I have no way of knowing that."

Lisa blew out an exasperated breath. "Listen, missy. I'm exercising every bit of control I can muster not to leap from this chair and run through the halls looking for Samantha. And now you tell me—"

The woman's jowls dropped. "I'm just the messenger."

"From where I sit, no news has been forthcoming," Lisa snapped.

"You don't need to raise your voice, ma'am."

Lisa sprang from her chair and leaned forward, hands pressed to the desk. She spoke in measured beats, reining herself in. "And you...don't...quite...seem...to understand...that I've lost a son. I can't lose my husband and daughter."

The woman adjusted her glasses and sat silent a moment. Finally, she spoke, her eyes fixed on her computer screen. "Your daughter's in the OR. You can wait in the family waiting room at the end of the hall. I'll page Dr. Hampton and let him know he can find you there."

Jake's head whipped skyward as Sam was ripped from his view. He scrambled to follow, but was momentarily blinded by the intense white light. Its sharpness sent him tumbling down the ladder as he futilely reached for the ladder rungs, which slipped repeatedly out of his grasp. The crackling noise grew louder...beeping...whirring... It sounded vaguely familiar, but Jake didn't think it was a short-wave radio. Jake's head's reeled as he realized he was failing his mission. He had to get Sam home.

He lunged back at the ladder, determined to climb it, but its steps rapidly withdrew just out of his reach—then the attic door slammed shut. A whoosh of warm air drifted down, headily scented with wildflowers.

"Bum luck."

Jake turned in shock, finding Jimmy standing in the doorway.

No. *No way.*

Chapter Eighteen

Lisa sat fidgeting in the waiting area, wishing she had something to do with her hands. Knitting. Anything. Instead, all she had nearby was a stack of last month's magazines. Gossip rags, the kind she rarely read, except when she was stuck in places like this. She picked one up and half-heartedly thumbed through it, barely absorbing the content. One pair of celebrities was getting divorced, another famous young person had undergone a public meltdown, and a royal family far away was having a baby.

Lisa flipped the magazine shut and closed her eyes, the memories crowding in on her. Sam had been such a beautiful child, right from the start. She'd had her daddy's eyes and a winning little-girl grin. While some mothers had difficulties with teenage daughters, Lisa had never had trouble with Sam. She'd been a happy and congenial kid who'd been fairly at peace among her small circle of friends. While she wasn't wildly outgoing like her brother, Sam had a solid sense of self and a quiet confidence in her art. She'd shown an aptitude in several media before finally finding her place in photography during college.

Because they thought more alike, Sam had naturally gravitated toward her father. She was inquisitive and entrepreneurial like he was. And as she grew into her career, the two of them became even closer than they'd been when Sam was a tiny thing riding on her daddy's shoulders. Lisa had a vision of them racing through the backyard, Ben carting Sam along toward the wheat fields. Sam used to squeal with glee, hanging on to the top of her Papa's head and calling him her "horsey." So many times Lisa had feared Sam might tumble off and get hurt, but she never had. Ben always held her securely.

"Mrs. Williams?"

Lisa opened her eyes to find Dr. Hampton standing before her. He was in scrubs with a surgical mask draped from his neck, as if he'd just emerged from surgery.

"Dr. Hampton, what is it?" Lisa rubbed her eyes. "Is Ben all right?"

"Better than all right." His brown eyes were intense, but his expression didn't change. "He's coming around."

"Around?" The fog in Lisa's brain cleared. "You mean, out of the anesthesia? But I thought you said—"

"It typically takes longer."

Lisa drew a hopeful breath. "Is this good news?"

"It's a very good sign."

Emotion overwhelmed her, striking like a tsunami. Lisa was generally good at keeping her feelings in, but so much had happened tonight she found self-restraint impossible. "Ben's not out of the woods yet," Dr. Hampton cautioned. But the way he said it gave every indication he believed Ben would be doing better soon.

Lisa leapt at the doctor and pulled him into a bear hug. "Thank you!" she blubbered, tears streaming from her eyes. The other families in the waiting area politely tried to appear disinterested. Dr. Hampton stiffened and lightly patted her back.

"Your husband's a fighter," he said when she released him. He adjusted his surgical mask, which Lisa's hug had skewed sideways. "He was very determined to come back for his family." His eyes creased when he smiled. "He was asking for you and his daughter."

"When can I see him?"

"Soon. We have to get him settled in the CICU, and the first visits will need to be brief." He nodded toward the elevator. "Why don't you wait about an hour, then come up to the third floor?"

Jake grabbed for the dangling cord and tugged on it hard.

Nothing budged.

He took it in two hands and tried again.

His muscles strained.

"No use trying." Jimmy sadly shook his head.

"Oh yes, there is," Jake said, throwing his weight into his work. Sweat beaded at his hairline and slicked the back of his neck. He wasn't giving up. Not now. This wasn't how things were supposed to go, he just knew it. It was an internal sense, a gut feeling. *I'm supposed to be with Sam.*

"Jake?" The woman's voice was soft and gentle.

His heart skipped a beat and for a second he swore it stopped pounding altogether.

"Come away from there, baby."

Jake's wet palms slid off the cord as he slowly turned to face her. Seconds before he met her light-green eyes, he knew who he would find. Carol Ann Ainsley. The woman he had loved and lost during the war. The one he'd proposed to on her birthday, and who'd been taken by a suicide bomber at a checkpoint just two days later.

Her pretty auburn hair was pulled back in a neat chignon. Her fair complexion held a gentle glow. She wore what he'd last seen her in: desert fatigues with a matching cap.

Jake was overwhelmed with love, loss, and longing. But most of all he felt a burning sensation in his heart: He had to get home.

Carol Ann held out her hand. "You're going the wrong way."

Dr. Hampton had barely departed the family waiting room when a woman arrived holding a clipboard. "Mrs. Williams?" she asked, her eyes surveying the pained faces crammed together in the small space.

"That's me," Lisa said, standing.

The woman approached her with brisk steps. She wore business attire and heels. A hospital ID badge dangled from a lanyard around her neck. "Emory Taylor," she said holding out her hand. "I'm the Patient Family Advocate for Blue Ridge Central."

"Yes?"

"I'm here with news about your daughter." She motioned to a couple of empty chairs in the corner, apart from where other family members waited. "Would you care to have a seat?"

Lisa set her jaw and steeled her heart.

"I think I'll stand."

Chapter Nineteen

Ten minutes earlier, a swirl of commotion had erupted in the operating room. A young patient named Samantha Williams had just undergone a sensitive surgery to reduce swelling in her brain. She'd also had a procedure to repair a collapsed lung. Though historically broken ribs were bandaged and set from the outside, it was later discovered the tight confines of any constraint prevented deep breathing, and so could lead to pneumonia. Now the ribs would have to heal on their own, and should repair themselves in due course—in roughly six weeks' time. The ankle that had been crushed when the steering column of her car collapsed downward had been splinted and set in a cast to give it extra help.

The poor child was a mess. Surgical nurse Kate Smith couldn't help but think of her own kids, and how horrific it would be to see one of them in this condition. Her girls were still in elementary school, but she was well aware that your kids never stopped being your kids no matter what their ages. Kate saw a lot of tragedy in this business and had endured her share of hard cases. The accident victims were always the worst. Like the poor guy who'd been pulled from the same scene, where he'd apparently been trying to save this female patient.

That was part of Kate's job now. The breathing tube had been removed from Sam's throat only minutes ago and Kate was monitoring how she was doing on the forced oxygen administered through small plastic tubes positioned by her nostrils. She said a silent prayer as she always did when she took a patient's post-op vitals. Then something totally unexpected happened. The moment she set her hand on Samantha's wrist, the girl's eyes popped open.

Sam stared in horror at the masked faces around her, not understanding where she was. Her throat felt ripped raw and her head throbbed so violently she feared it would burst into a billion pieces. Machinery clicked and beeped around her. *The radio.* She moved her mouth and tried to speak, but her lips were sandpaper-dry.

"Doctor!" Kate called and another woman turned. By the other woman's stance it was clear she was in charge.

"Get Dr. Carter back here stat," the woman commanded, before leaning over Sam. "Samantha?" she said gently. "Can you hear me?"

Sam tried to focus on their faces, but her world was growing foggy again, the bright lights growing dim.

Dr. Carter bustled in, checking Sam's pulse, her eye on the monitors.

"I think you'd better go and get the mom," Dr. Carter told Kate.

Sam saw she was hooked up to an IV and felt faint. Then she thought of Jake—where was he?

Jake swallowed hard and glanced around the room. Jimmy was nowhere in sight.

He'd loved Carol Ann. Loved her madly. But that was a long time ago and now his life held another purpose.

"Jake," Carol Ann said, "I've been waiting for you. A lot of us have."

Jake's mind raced back over the events of the past several hours. His SUV running off the road...encountering Sam's accident...helping her reach Becky's Diner and then coming here. But this couldn't be the end of his journey.

Part of him wanted to take Carol Ann in his arms and hold her, like he'd dreamed of doing so many times. When she'd gone, he'd kept a stiff upper lip in public. But deep inside he'd been battling despair. He'd become inconsolable, despondent. In the dark of night, he'd let the tears stream onto his pillow, but had held his breath so his ragged sobs wouldn't wake his bunkmates. Jake hadn't understood what it meant to have a broken heart until then. And once he'd experienced it, he'd become committed to preventing himself from experiencing that torture again.

Yet all he wanted now was to live, to dare himself to test that capacity for emotion once more. The truth hit in a lightning bolt of understanding.

With Sam.

Carol Ann took a step toward him, her arms outstretched.

But Jake froze in place.

Not six inches above him sat that old attic door.

Light still burned through its edges.

Chapter Twenty

Lisa stood by the hospital gurney holding Sam's hand. Her daughter was flitting in and out of consciousness. Still groggy, but coming around. Sam's eyelids fluttered open and she gave Lisa a wan smile. "Hi, Mom." Tears of gratitude burned trails down Lisa's cheeks. She lifted a sweater sleeve to dry them, not daring to release Sam's hand. "How's Dad?"

"Holding up like a trouper." Lisa forced a shaky smile. "Just like you."

"I'm sorry about all this."

"For goodness' sake," Lisa jumped in, "don't apologize. I'm just so thankful that—"

Worry lines creased Sam's forehead. "Does Papa know?"

Lisa tried to focus on Sam's eyes and not the multitude of tubes and monitor wires that threaded around her. "Not yet. He's just been moved to his room."

Sam smiled wryly. "I got here just in time."

"I would have liked it so much better if you hadn't arrived by ambulance."

"I know."

She seemed to be drifting off again, her eyelids heavy. "Jimmy... He..."

Lisa caught her breath. "Jimmy?"

"I...saw him."

No, Lisa thought, that couldn't be! That would have to mean that Sam... Another heavy tear slid down Lisa's cheek. She'd heard of those things happening, of loved ones coming to meet you when you crossed over to the other side, but never had been sure whether to believe them.

Sam squeezed Lisa's hand, speaking with labored breaths. "He said, 'Tell Mama I'm okay.'"

Lisa's eyes burned hot and her throat swelled shut. She tried to swallow, but she couldn't. The lump in her throat was too large and tender.

Sam mumbled something more, but the words were mangled. Dr. Carter had told Lisa that would happen as the anesthesia wore off and the painkillers took over. Lisa wondered if the tale about Jimmy had something to do with the medication, though her heart hoped otherwise. Not that she'd ever wish her daughter to be in mortal danger, but the very thought that her son had tried to reach her... It was incredible. And, in an inexplicable way, the idea—even if it *was* some sort of delusion—provided her with an enormous sense of peace. A peace Lisa hadn't felt since she first learned of Jimmy's disappearance near the Baltic Sea.

Lisa found her voice to ask, "What is it, darling? What did you say?"

Sam struggled for alertness, puffing out the word: "Jake."

Jake Marlow, that's who Sam was asking about. The Good Samaritan who'd come to her aid. When the hospital social worker spoke to Lisa, she'd helped patch together a picture of what had happened, based on reports from the EMT crew and news from state troopers. Sam had apparently lost control of her car and skidded into a ditch. The police located another vehicle abandoned on the same stretch of road. The registration papers matched the ID on the man they found with Sam. The one who'd apparently risked his life to pull her from a burning car, then had shielded her body from the jettisoning debris when the engine exploded. He'd protected her from going into shock and had lent her his body warmth, even when his was slipping away.

"I need to see him. Help him. I promised..."

A nurse was walking toward Lisa now, indicating it was time to leave. She'd been told she could come back and check on Sam in another hour.

"You just rest now, honey," Lisa said. "I'll be back soon."

"But Jake."

"I know. It's a miracle he was there. We're a lot in his debt."

And in Ben's, Lisa realized suddenly. If Ben hadn't signaled for Jake to drive over this evening, he might not have found Sam. And if Jake hadn't found Sam... Lisa's heart ached. She couldn't bear to think of that scenario. It was hard enough facing the one in front of her. But Sam was going to be okay. Her little girl was going to make it. Ben's situation seemed to be improving too. Tragically, things didn't look as good for Jake.

"I need to see him, Mama," Sam said her voice growing throaty. "Say thank you..."

"Of course, honey." The last thing Lisa wanted to do now was burden her injured daughter with unhappy news. "When you're better." She smiled tenderly at

Sam and gently stroked her hair, until the tightness of Sam's grip released and she fell back to sleep.

A little while later, Lisa was upstairs with Ben.

"Where is she?" he challenged groggily. "I woke up thinking of her. It was almost like...something was wrong."

Lisa met his eyes. "You and Sam always did have a connection."

Ben glanced through the glass window out into the hall. "She's not here yet? I thought she would have—"

"I don't want you to worry, because Sam's okay."

Ben lurched forward, the cord on his IV pulled tight. "What's going on?" Heart monitors kicked up, registering a staccato beat.

"Sweetheart, please. Now, don't get excited."

A nurse tore into the room, checking her instruments. She gave Lisa a quick once-over. "What happened in here?"

Lisa drew a breath. "I was just telling Ben about our daughter."

The nurse's face flushed and she lowered her chin. Apparently everyone in the hospital had heard about it by now, this double tragedy striking the same family in one night. She checked the flow of the IV, then quietly addressed Lisa. "Maybe any long conversations should wait."

"I will not have you two talking around me like I'm some kind of infant!" Ben grumbled. "If something's happened with Sam, I want to know what it is."

The nurse shot Lisa a warning glance, but Lisa pressed ahead. She simply couldn't keep this from Ben. Were the circumstances reversed, she'd never want him to keep things from her, especially if it concerned their child.

The nurse unclipped the chart from the foot of Ben's bed and began making notes. She obviously wasn't leaving and Ben's agitation was increasing.

"You'll need to sit back, Mr. Williams," the nurse told him. "Take some deep breaths. I can give you more pain medication in a few minutes, and something to help you sleep."

"Like hell," he said stormily before turning to Lisa. Lisa sank under the weight of his stare.

Lisa spoke calmly in an even tone. "She's going to be okay, Ben. Sam had a little accident..."

Monitor readings soared again.

"Breathe," the nurse instructed.

Ben sucked in some air through his teeth. "A car accident?"

"Yes, but she's fine."

"Because of me?" His chin trembled, then he added with understanding, "She was rushing to get home for my surgery."

The nurse locked eyes with Lisa. "I'm going to step out and get his meds. I'll page Dr. Hampton to come look in on him when you're done."

"Thank you," Lisa said sincerely.

"But please," the nurse pressed, "just five more minutes."

Lisa nodded, then took Ben's hand above the mass of tubing. "Sam took some hard knocks, but she's going to make it. She's a fighter just like you."

Ben set his jaw but his eyes watered. "How bad is it, Lisa? Tell me."

"She's pulled through the worst of it. Surgery."

Ben squeezed his eyes shut. "No."

"Successful, Dr. Carter said."

Ben's eyes flipped open. He stared at her, agape. "Elizabeth Carter?"

"Why, yes."

"She's top-notch."

"How do you know?"

"I used to know her mother."

"That's funny. You never mentioned it."

"It was a long time ago."

Chapter Twenty-One

It was the blizzard of the century and no one in this part of the state had seen it coming. But when the arctic blast hit that fast-moving front, two feet of snow blanketed western Virginia. Ben was in his third year of college and thankful to have chains on the tires of his truck. No one else was fool enough to brave this road under such dangerous conditions, but there was a blond, dark-eyed girl Ben needed to see. Forget all the fancy stuff he'd learned in astronomy. *His* sun rose and set in Lisa. He was going to marry that girl someday, once he figured out how to earn enough money.

She was studying at another school, three hundred miles away, but he took every opportunity he could to go see her. This weekend was more special than most. It was her birthday and he'd made her a surprise: a dark-chocolate birthday cake from scratch. No way was he going to mess up delivering that. He hoped it would taste as good as it looked, and his roommate's girlfriend (who'd shared the recipe) assured him it would.

Ben couldn't wait to see Lisa's face when she got it. Dark chocolate was her favorite. Plus she'd teased him mercilessly about his lack of cooking skills. And here he'd gone and done it! He'd pulled off baking an entire dessert, and was fast on the way to proving himself a modern man.

Ben cranked up the radio to combat the rash of loneliness that accompanied this journey. It was a five-hour drive in each direction. He wouldn't have undertaken it for any other girl. Afternoon was settling in and the sky grew dark above the slanting snow that pummeled his windshield. That's when he passed it: a broken-down Camaro sitting on the side of the road. Ben slowed and checked his rearview mirror. He hadn't been mistaken. There was a woman sitting inside it.

Ben steered his truck onto the shoulder and raced back toward the car. No one stopped anywhere like this unless there was an emergency. The woman had seen him coming and rolled down her driver's side window. "Thank goodness you pulled over." Her breath fogged the chilly air. In her right hand she clutched one of those new car phones Ben had heard about. "My engine overheated, and I can't get this darn thing to work." She shook the handset in her grip. "Some newfangled thing my daughter gave me."

Ben was a smart guy, but he wasn't sure he knew how to work it either. It seemed they were in the middle of nowhere. "Can I give you a lift somewhere? Maybe if you get to a real phone, you can send back for your car?"

She gave him a grateful smile. "I'd hate to put you to any trouble."

"No trouble. I'm going your way."

"I haven't even told you which way that is."

Ben hardly saw how that mattered. He certainly wasn't going to leave a middle-aged woman sitting alone in a disabled car.

He smiled with good humor. "What are your choices?"

She nodded her assent. "Seems I'm out of options."

On the way to her house, Ben learned all about Miss Beulah. She'd lost her husband in Vietnam, but had a daughter, Elizabeth, a promising young medical student who was going to do great things for this world. It was obvious Miss Beulah was very proud of her. Ben supposed she had every reason to be. He'd briefly considered a medical career himself, but the pull of the stars had been too great. Perhaps someday he'd do something to benefit medicine. He wasn't quite sure how, but that evening he put it on his agenda. Many of the scientific fields overlapped in certain obscure ways. Perhaps one day he'd invent something that could also be of use to a doctor like Miss Beulah's daughter. He told her this and she laughed. But her laugh was genuine and warm. "You have ambition, I see."

"A little," Ben admitted, underplaying it.

"Sounds like there's a girl in the picture."

"Might be."

"Well, good for you." She chuckled. "Don't mess it up."

Ben was taken aback by her candor, but also charmed by it. "Believe me, I don't intend to."

"So have you asked her?"

Ben nearly choked on his answer. "Beg pardon?"

"Well, go on." Miss Beulah grinned as big as all get-out. Ben had to fight to keep his eyes on the road. "What are you waiting for?"

"To finish my education. Get a stable job."

"Ah, phooey! If there's one thing I can tell you, it's you never know what the future holds. When you see something that's right, you grab it with both hands. You're a handsome young man, clearly intelligent. Surely you can see the wisdom in that?"

They chatted a bit longer about this and that, the crazy weather and current events. But mostly, Miss Beulah seemed interested in talking about Ben. He supposed she must get lonely living in such a rural area. When he asked about her closest neighbor, she'd replied with a chuckle, "What's a neighbor?"

Ben dropped her at her door and she thanked him for his help.

"I never forget a kindness."

Ben felt a tad guilty leaving her there all alone. Even though it was her house and the electricity appeared to be running, she was miles from any town. She told him not to worry, and that she was used to living this way. Made her feel independent.

She wrapped her shawl around herself and scurried through the snow. Ben watched from his truck until she reached the front door of her house and entered safely. That was the last he'd seen of Miss Beulah, though his visit with her had clearly left its mark.

Even after all this time, he believed he was the one in her debt. Her advice had shaken him to his core. Not because he hadn't thought about it, but because he hadn't intended to act on it so soon. But Miss Beulah was right. If he knew Lisa was who he wanted, wouldn't it be better for them to get started on their future plans sooner rather than later?

Many times after, Ben had secretly thanked Miss Beulah for her interference. If she hadn't prodded him to do what he'd privately yearned to do, he might not have proposed to Lisa that snowy weekend, and then they wouldn't have had Jimmy nine months later.

What's more, his precious Sam wouldn't have been born.

Ben had never told Lisa about helping Miss Beulah in the storm that night, mostly because he hadn't wanted her to know that his idea to propose that weekend hadn't been entirely his own. But the fact was that the chance encounter with a stranded middle-aged woman on a lonely highway had changed Ben's life for the better. Now, in an incredible twist of fate, Miss Beulah's daughter had stepped forward to help him.

He'd kept track of Elizabeth Carter's career, but only obliquely. He'd seen her written up in the papers, and in a few medical journals he read as a hobby. Elizabeth Carter was a respected trauma specialist who could have practiced anywhere. In deference to her mother and others like her who were committed to living in this rugged land, Dr. Carter opted to stay in Virginia and serve those in the most remote regions of the state. Those who might need top-notch medical care for a severe emergency, but who didn't have the luxury of time or money to get transported to a higher-tier hospital. Miss Beulah, God rest her soul, had passed some years ago. But her legacy lived on in her daughter, a caring and accomplished surgeon who spent more time at the hospital than she did at home, according to the staff that revered her.

Her nearly flawless record of saving patients was legendary. When asked how it was possible she'd saved so many lives, particularly when some of the situations seemed hopeless, she'd answered the reporter with a laugh, saying perhaps she had help from the other side. When he'd read that article, Ben had thought Dr. Carter to be joking, or that she was merely trying to deflect some of the attention from herself. Now, Ben found himself wondering what the real truth was. Not that he was the sort to believe in ghosts.

"Ben? Are you all right?" He looked into his wife's eyes, not sure how long he'd been away caught up in his reverie.

"Yes, Lisa. I'm here."

"Good, because the nurse says I need to leave now."

Ben glanced at the door and saw his nurse had reappeared, carting a tray holding a small syringe.

Lisa lightly kissed his forehead. "Be good, and get better."

"That's my plan," he said, meaning it absolutely.

Chapter Twenty-Two

Jake could hear Sam's voice calling him, but it was far away.

"Jake..." Carol Ann stepped closer, her arms lowered to her sides, her palms upturned. "All you have to do is accept it."

Accept it? Like he could accept that Sam was meant to perish in that burning car? Jake's senses were too keen for him to ignore them. They'd shielded him from trouble his whole life, and had helped him keep Sam out of harm's way. When he'd vowed to protect her, she'd promised him something in return. What was it?

I'm here for you too.

Jake's heart thudded, then it pounded harder.

Wham! Something slammed his chest with a sizzle.

No, a volt.

A hundred volts.

Three thousand.

Oh, man. That hurt!

His sweater was on fire.

Or maybe he was dreaming it.

"Jake!" Carol Ann rushed toward him, but he recoiled.

Her lips were tinged blue. "I love you."

"I'll always love you," he told her. "But I can't stay."

Then he lunged for the dangling cord.

"Again!" the doc called in the emergency room, pressing the defibrillator to Jake's chest. "We're not going to lose him!"

Jake's back arched beneath him, his chest rearing toward the ceiling like a bronco. Light flooded the room, assaulting Jake's eyes. Then he caught his breath. A choking breath that burned and pulled at his lungs, threatening to tear his insides apart with searing pain.

A masked surgeon placed her gloved hand on the shoulder of another physician in front of her. "Nice job, Dr. Carter."

Jake struggled to see their faces, but everything went black.

When Jake next opened his eyes, he found Sam sitting beside him. Her face was bruised and her head bandaged, but she was as beautiful as ever.

Monitors went haywire and nurses sped into the room.

"Welcome back," Mr. Williams said. Jake stared at the man he'd come over the mountain to see. The client, who'd been on his deathbed, was dressed in a robe and slippers. He sat in a chair beside a walker, but was apparently now moving about on his own.

"You're okay?"

"The surgery was successful," Sam's dad replied. "They're discharging me next week."

Sam held Jake's gaze as medical personnel flurried around him, checking his stats and taking his pulse.

Jake wasn't sure how his heart could beat any more fiercely. His thoughts raced, taking his new reality in. *I'm here. With Sam.*

She gently took his hand. "You gave us quite a scare."

Jake tried to raise his head off the pillow, but it throbbed, so he laid it back down. "I don't understand."

"You inhaled a lot of smoke when you pulled me from my car," Sam explained. "The carbon monoxide was too much. It got into your bloodstream and worked its way to your heart. But all that time, your only thought was keeping me safe."

The head nurse indicated all looked good and that she was going to notify the doctor. She grinned at Jake as she left. "We'll have you up and out of here in no time."

Jake's eyes traveled the room, taking in floral arrangements of assorted seasonal bouquets, even a vase of roses. "How long have I been out?"

"A couple of days," Sam replied. "The flowers are from the folks in your office. Your parents sent the roses. They wanted you to know they're on their way."

Jake nodded, vaguely recalling his mom had been on an art retreat in Italy, and that his dad had joined her on the trip. He hated that they'd cut their travels short on account of him, though it sure felt good to know they were coming.

It was only then that Jake noticed Sam was in a wheelchair, dressed in hospital attire. "What about you? Are you—?"

"I'm going to be fine." She smiled softly. "Thanks to you." Sam nodded toward an older woman seated in the corner. "Jake, this is my mom."

"All of us were very concerned," Lisa said. She had blond hair like Sam and light-brown eyes. "Ben and I can't thank you enough for what you did for our daughter."

"Of course." His voice cracked, his throat still burning. Jake felt a pang in his chest and drew his free hand to it. "My heart? Did it...?"

"Your heart stopped beating briefly in the OR," Sam told him, "but they brought you back."

"*Dr. Carter* brought you back," Mrs. Williams said with emphasis.

"Yes," Mr. Williams added before clearing his throat. "And as soon as you're out of that bed, I'm going to need some legal advice."

"Papa!" Sam protested.

Jake laughed, the rumbling motion causing another ache in his chest, but he didn't care. He was here, in the light of day, with Sam.

"I had the weirdest dream," he told her. "About you and me."

Her cheeks colored sweetly. "I had it, too. Only..."

"What?"

"I've figured a few things out."

"That so?"

"Like where Becky's Diner came from."

"Becky's Diner?" Sam's parents asked together.

"Say," Sam's mom said. "Wasn't Becky the name of that EMT who—?"

"Doesn't matter," Sam told them. "A lot of it's growing foggy anyway."

Jake locked on her eyes and smiled. "Yeah."

She was gorgeous sitting there beside him. Gorgeous and just as warm and good-hearted as Jake remembered when he'd thought he heard Sam calling him from the other side. Who knew? Maybe she had been beckoning him here, and—apart from Dr. Carter's skill—that's what brought him back. Jake decided then and there not to tell Sam about seeing Carol Ann. He might let her know about his past involvement someday, but there was no point in sharing that Carol Ann had tried to keep him in the hereafter. Jake didn't blame her for it. Carol Ann was in a better place and wanted to welcome him to that world too. The only thing was, Jake wasn't ready.

He wanted to stay here in this dimension with Sam. And they were going to have a future together. Without a doubt, Jake knew this in his soul. Now, all he had to do was ask her on a date.

Chapter Twenty-Three

One month later, Jake sat opposite Sam at the Mountain View Diner.

She lifted her fork and grinned. "I think it's pretty fitting you asked me out for apple pie."

Jake dug into his own generous wedge, thinking it smelled delicious. It was nice and hot too, its apple-cinnamon aroma filling the air. "A fitting way to celebrate, you mean."

"I'm so proud of my dad," Sam said. "His invention will help so many people."

"I didn't even realize he'd had an earlier interest in medicine."

"Now he has a way to benefit both fields."

Jake took a sip of coffee. "Lots of fields."

Sam clinked her mug to his. "Yeah."

"So," he asked her in between bites, "how are things going at the studio?"

"Arghh." Sam gritted her teeth in frustration. "They're still trying to throw us out."

"But they can't do that. Not until the end of your year."

"McAdams is threatening to," she said referring to the businessman leading the charge. Jake had heard of him and didn't care much for his tactics. He also wasn't fond of the firm representing him. He preferred entities like his own that actually backed the arts. The senior partners at his firm regularly provided endowments to the arts community. Once Jake was promoted—and he was hoping that someday soon he would be—Jake planned to carry on that tradition. Maybe he could start by offering a bit of help now.

"I could take a look at your lease if you'd like," he offered.

"But I thought real estate isn't your specialty?"

"The law is the law." Jake shot her a wink. "I know how to read the fine print."

Sam heaved a sigh. "That would be terrific. If I at least had until the end of the year, I'd have time to devise another plan. Find an alternate space."

Jake shared a confident grin. "Maybe you won't have to."

Sam ducked her head with a blush. She'd never met a guy willing to do so many nice things for her, even go out on a limb professionally. When she looked up, he was gazing at her in a way that made her temperature spike and her heart beat faster.

His dark eyes twinkled. "You healed up pretty well. Not even a scar."

Sam pulled the bangs back at her hairline to reveal a jagged purple line. "May have this one for a while."

Jake reached over and trailed a finger across it. His touch was warm and gentle, reminding her of being in his arms. "It suits you. It will help us remember."

"I don't remember much," she admitted. "I felt so lost, like I was in a fog."

"That's because you were."

"But you were there with me."

He spoke with his eyes on hers. "Never left your side."

Sam knew that Becky was the lead EMT who'd cared for them and gotten them into their separate ambulances. A passing trucker had spied smoke coming from the ditch and called 9-1-1 on his CB radio. And all those lights they'd thought they'd seen? Those had to have been from when help had arrived on the scene, or maybe from an examination light inside the ambulance, or at the hospital—much like the way that real-world externalities sometimes become incorporated into dreams.

They'd had a sense of light coming from somewhere, and were driven to pursue it. Perhaps that's what's meant by "having a will to live." While they were still in the hospital, she and Jake had discussed all this and put most of it together.

What neither understood was how their delusions had been so similar. When Sam mentioned this again, Jake said, "You know, I've been thinking about that, and I guess it's possible we were communicating somehow."

"You mean like talking in our sleep?"

"We had to pass the time under that tree somehow." Jake chuckled, and she liked the way his eyes danced when he did. They were spectacular eyes: dark and soulful. Sam felt as if she'd seen into Jake's soul in a very special way.

"You passed it pretty well taking care of me. Dr. Carter said if it hadn't been for—"

"Hey." His expression was sincere. "Let's not go there, all right? I did what any man would have done."

"No," she said firmly. "You did what *Jake Marlow* would have done. You can say what you want, but you're a hero in my book. In my mom and dad's eyes, too."

A smile creased the corners of his lips. "From where I sit, you saved me. It was your voice that called me back, and the thought of being with you. Like we are right here."

He met her eyes and Sam's heart fluttered. When they'd discussed their travels through the fog, they'd compared notes on many things. On everything but that kiss. Now, Sam found herself wondering if that had even happened. She was too embarrassed to mention it, particularly as she'd been the one to put the moves on Jake. Perhaps she'd only imagined that event, and it hadn't happened at all.

"I think it's pretty cool that your dad knew Miss Beulah," he said. "I mean, way back when."

"And that Dr. Carter is her daughter," Sam replied, reiterating what her dad had shared with them and Lisa earlier.

"That part's a little freaky," Jake admitted.

"Not as freaky as us both remembering being there."

"In Miss Beulah's house," Jake affirmed.

"Apparently, she's been gone a long time. The house was demolished years ago." Sam paused and bit her lip. After a beat, she asked, "You don't suppose that she...? Miss Beulah could have somehow helped—?"

"Come on, we never even saw her. I mean, I didn't. Did you?"

Sam slumped back against her booth. "No, only Jimmy."

An image of her brother sprang to mind, and her eyes welled with tears.

"I'm sorry, Sam."

"No, don't be." She smiled softly at the memory. "It was so good to see him. Only, now that's fading away too. It's like it was clear in the beginning, but now, well... Sometimes I wonder about what I really remember."

"I know, I feel that way too. At first, everything was so sharp. But now, it's becoming a blur. It could be we were on some sort of cusp. In a realm we're not meant to understand."

"Or even know about," Sam agreed. Her eyes searched his. She could scarcely accept the truth. "Your heart stopped for two minutes," she said, repeating what the doctors told her.

"You were right on the brink yourself."

"But we came back."

Jake reached across the table and took her hand. "You came back first, and after you did..." Sam's face warmed. "I knew I had to come back with you.

"Sam," he said, his voice raspy. "You and I... It's about more than the accident."

Sam swallowed hard, forcing the words past the rawness in her throat. "I sense that too."

"I think we should give it a try, get to know each other. Because what I've seen so far, I certainly like a lot. For the most part, we've been hospital patients, or strangers with a run of bad luck."

"I wouldn't say our luck was all bad."

"No, we caught some mighty fine breaks. I'll always be grateful for those, and to the people who took care of us when we couldn't take care of ourselves."

"The way you took care of me."

"The point is..." He paused a moment as his Adam's apple rose and fell. "That apart from what we've been through, or maybe because of it, I believe there's something good here, something great between the two of us. In my estimation, it could be wonderful. Because gosh-darn-it, Sam." He drew a breath and appeared to steel himself, dark eyes brimming. "I really like you."

Sam nodded, and a tear escaped her. It was as if all his words were expressing her thoughts as well, and each had come from his heart. She spoke, her lips trembling, barely able to contain her emotions. "I like you too," she uttered, knowing deep inside that the word *like* wasn't strong enough.

Jake raised his hand to cup her cheek and Sam's skin tingled beneath his touch. "Even though the dream is fading," he whispered, "there's one thing I can't forget." Sam's breath caught and her heart pounded as his mouth moved in. He leaned toward her with his revelation, a smile tickling the edge of his lips. "I like the way you kiss."

Sam gasped with surprise, mortified that he remembered. Then, at once, sheer joy overtook her when she realized what he meant. He hadn't been put off by her advances. In fact, it appeared he hoped to encourage them again. She'd never been as attracted to a man as she was to Jake. She'd never *wanted* a man as badly as she did Jake. *To have and to hold from this day forward,* chimed a tiny voice in her head. Sam didn't know if that was her heart talking, or a little old lady matchmaker giving her a nudge. Either way, she was glad she'd only thought it, and that Jake hadn't heard.

His lips brushed hers, their pressure warm and tender, his kiss revealing more than words could say. There was so much neither understood, but in some ways it was as if their souls *knew.* Like the two of them fit, and were fated to be together.

Jake cradled her face in his hands and kissed her again, until Sam's cheeks burned hot and her spirit soared. When he pulled back, he grinned. "I don't know where we go from here. You've already taken me to heaven."

Sam tugged him toward her, sighing as she did. To her way of thinking, that was a trip meant for two. She brought her mouth to his with a breathy whisper: "Maybe I should take you there again." Then she kissed him back with everything she had, for Jake was her man, her future…her destiny. She felt this with every fiber of her being.

Who knew where they'd been, really? Some place far from here, the memory of which was already fading fast. Two things were clear: The emotion that burned between them, and the heat of Jake's kiss. Nothing else mattered and it was as if no one else was there. In her mind's eye, and in her heart, all Sam saw was Jake.

He'd stepped out of the fog to take her in his arms.

Now they were embracing the world together.

Epilogue

The following Christmas there was a new engagement to celebrate at the Williams house. Lisa carted a tray of eggnog into the living room and served a glass to each member of the family, reserving the one without bourbon for Ben. He'd been a model patient during his recovery and now took very particular care of his health. He had so many positives to focus on, and was lecturing widely on his new find.

Sam and Jake joined hands on the sofa and a diamond glistened on Sam's left hand. Lisa had never seen her daughter looking so lovely, or so happy. Jake had popped the question the week before, after surprising Sam with the news that his firm had completely thwarted the attempted takeover of the arts district and her gallery. Some very powerful political figures were involved, all of whom valued culture over questionable "progress."

Ben raised his glass and smiled. "What shall we drink to this year?"

Jake shot Sam a loving look. "I already got my wish."

She whispered back sweetly, "Me too."

Lisa's heart warmed as she recalled what it was like to be young and in love. Sam and Jake were so well suited to each other. She and Ben took comfort in knowing Sam couldn't have found a better man.

In some ways, Lisa had received everything she'd hoped for too. Her Ben was getting better, and Samantha had fully recovered. This year Lisa knew that when she packed the holiday decorations away, every candle would be taken from its window. Because in her heart, she now believed that Jimmy had also finally found his way home.

Jake offered a suggestion. "How about we drink to the North Star?"

Ben's brow rose with interest. "The North Star, huh?"

Jake nodded and squeezed Sam's hand. "It helped bring us home."

Sam leaned into him and they exchanged glances like they shared some kind of secret. When Sam turned back to her dad, tears glistened in her eyes. "It was your love, Papa." She quickly looked at Lisa. "And yours too. The whole time it was leading me."

"Like Sam called me," Jake said firmly. He wrapped an arm around his new fiancée, holding her close. "Love *is* a guiding light."

Lisa surveyed the pair with affection, thinking what a handsome couple they made. Beyond them, snow fell lightly outside the window, streaking the darkness with wisps of white. The candle on the windowsill glowed brightly, sending glimmers of warmth into the night.

Silence fell over the room as they absorbed Jake's words. It was true and Lisa knew it. As long as you let its light in, love could take you where you needed to go.

It had brought Sam home and brought a new son into the family. It had also helped her make peace with Jimmy's loss, even after all this time.

Ben nodded his agreement and raised his glass. "To the North Star!" he croaked hoarsely. "And its light!"

"Here, here!" they all shouted. Then they smiled and toasted each other, laughing and sighing over the trials and accomplishments of the year, each knowing things could only get better. They'd already come this far.

The End

A Note from the Author

Thanks for reading *The Light at the End of the Road*. I hope you enjoyed it. If you did, please help other people find this book.

1. This book is lendable, so send it to a friend you think might like it so that she (or he) can discover my work too.

2. Help other people find this book: Write a review.

3. Sign up for my newsletter so you can learn about the next book as soon as it's available. Write to GinnyBairdRomance@gmail.com with "newsletter" in the subject heading.

4. Come like my Facebook page: https://www.facebook.com/GinnyBairdRomance.

5. Connect with me on Twitter: https://twitter.com/GinnyBaird.

6. Visit my website at http://www.ginnybairdromance.com for details on other books now available at multiple outlets.

If you enjoy romantic ghost stories, you might like *The Ghost Next Door (A Love Story)*. Keep reading for an excerpt here.

Ginny Baird's

The Ghost Next Door (A Love Story)

A single mom and her teenage daughter move next to a spooky old house, and the small-town sheriff comes to their aid.

Chapter One

Elizabeth set her hand on her hip and gazed out over the countryside. She and Claire stood by their silver SUV, parked at the top of the steep gravel drive.

"Thought you said it had a view."

She glanced at the fifteen-year-old girl beside her with long, brown hair and bangs. Dark eyes brimmed with dramatic expression.

"Jeez, Mom. You didn't say it was of a graveyard."

"Cemetery."

"What?"

"Graveyards are beside a church. Cemeteries are stand-alone—"

Claire's jaw dropped in disbelief. "If you're such a stickler for words, why didn't you read the fine print?"

"What fine print?"

"The one saying we'd be moving next to a haunted house?"

Elizabeth's gaze traveled to the run-down Victorian less than a stone's throw from the modern, prefab house they'd rented. She figured the land the newer house stood on had once belonged to the larger home, which now sat with murky windows, sunshine reflecting off of beveled glass. Its wide front porch was caked with dust, gnarly vines tangling their way around paint-cracked spindles holding the porch railings.

Elizabeth chided herself for not investigating further when the ad said Bucolic, small-town setting. Unobstructed mountain views. She hadn't known those views would be peppered with tombstones, or that they'd be living beside an empty house.

"Maybe it won't be so bad?" she offered hopefully.

A sharp wind blew, sending the twin rockers on the Victorian's front porch sighing as they heaved to and fro as if tipped by some unseen hand.

Claire frowned, turning away. "It's creepy. This whole place is creepy. I don't think we should stay."

A tension in Elizabeth's gut told her perhaps Claire was right. Even the rocking chairs tilting in the wind seemed a bad omen. But a greater tension in her wallet said she'd already signed a lease for the next nine months. There'd be no backing out of it without losing her security deposit plus the first month's rent.

Elizabeth drew a breath, studying the more positive parts of the landscape. The two-story place they'd rented appeared almost new, with a cheery front garden and a covered stoop. Its clapboard siding and slate roof were well kept, giving the home a cottagey feel. And the large side yard housed a sturdy oak, its leaves shimmering orangey gold in the October sun. "The setting may be a little unusual," she told her daughter, "but at least it's quiet."

"Yeah. Dead quiet."

"Come on," Elizabeth urged. "Help me get the groceries in the house. Then we can grab our luggage. We'll be settled in no time." She flashed the girl a grin. "Spaghetti for dinner."

Claire shrugged and reluctantly reached into the hatchback for some bags. "Whatever."

Later that night, as she and Claire stood drying dishes by the sink, Elizabeth questioned her wisdom in bringing them here. This rental property was pretty isolated, at least five miles from the tiny village nearby. But when she'd been searching for a temporary place for them to stay, there hadn't been a lot of options. Blayton, Virginia was so small it wasn't even on most maps. Set up against the Blue Ridge Mountains, it had once been an old railroad town, the gateway community between here and Tennessee on the far side of those high peaks. After a period of anonymity, it was now undergoing a minor renaissance, with a new microbrewery moving in, a few swank restaurants, and a burgeoning host of surrounding vineyards and upscale B&Bs. Though trains no longer stopped here, the working tracks remained intact, with the original station now converted into the local library.

Elizabeth had been sent here to revamp the old town newspaper, previously called the Gazette. Her larger news organization was intent on acquiring antiquated or defunct town papers and bringing their newer incarnations into the twenty-first century. Elizabeth had fought this relocation, begging her boss in Richmond to let her tackle this from afar. After all, the real focus of all their newer editions was virtual subscriptions offered on the Internet. But Jerry had argued she needed to be on the scene, get up close and personal with the local community to make this transition work. Besides, he persisted, in order for the new publication to be successful, it needed to develop ground legs too. Perhaps a younger readership might emerge online, but for the old-timers to get roped in, there had to be a physical edition of the paper as well. Something folks could pick up at the local grocery, which was extra convenient since there was only one store in town.

"Mom, look!" Claire's eyes went wide as the dish she was drying slipped from her hands. It collided with the linoleum at her feet and split in two.

Elizabeth stepped toward her daughter. "Honey, what's wrong?"

"Did... Did you see it?" Claire stammered.

She followed Claire's gaze out the kitchen window to the house across the way. Evening shadows shrouded the Victorian, its windows dark and dreary.

"Up there." She pointed to a window on the second floor. "I saw something move inside."

Elizabeth wrapped her arm around Claire's shoulder, thinking the day was getting to her. It had been a five-hour drive from Richmond, then there'd been unpacking to do. It was unnerving to be a teen and move far from your school and long-term friends. It had to be doubly upsetting to find your new home situated across the street from a cemetery. The poor kid was tired and overwrought, letting her imagination get the best of her. And Claire had quite an imagination. She'd taken first prize in her district's teen short-story contest and had recently turned her storytelling ability into songwriting while she plucked out accompanying music on her secondhand guitar.

"I'm sure it was nothing," Elizabeth told her. "Maybe just a shadow from the big oak outside."

Claire narrowed her eyes in thought. "Yeah, maybe." She bent to grab the broken dish, and Elizabeth stooped to help her.

"Here, let me get this. Why don't you go grab the broom and dustpan from over there in the corner?"

After the two of them had cleaned up, they once more stood by the sink and stared out the window.

"I'm sure it was just a shadow," Elizabeth said.

"You're probably right."

Just then a beam of light swept through the big house's downstairs, and Claire leapt into Elizabeth's arms. "Mo-om!"

Elizabeth held her tightly. "Hang on, I'm sure it's just a—"

"A what?" Elizabeth's pulse raced. "You said the house was empty! For sale!"

"Maybe it's a potential buyer?" Elizabeth said lamely, not for a second believing that was true. Who on earth visited creepy old houses as night fell? Maybe someone who worked during the day and couldn't get here otherwise, Elizabeth told herself logically. Just look at her, gripping her daughter like she was some freaked-out kid herself. Elizabeth knew better than that.

"Is it gone?" Claire asked, her eyes tightly shut.

Elizabeth returned her gaze to the window and the looming house next door. There wasn't a hint of movement anywhere. "No signs of life."

Claire popped both eyes open. "I wish you hadn't said that."

Just then the doorbell rang with a spooky twang, and Elizabeth yelped.

"Ow, Mom! What are you doing? It's just the front door."

Elizabeth released her grasp, feeling foolish. "Of course it is," she replied in an even tone. But they weren't expecting company and were miles from anywhere.

The doorbell chimed again, and Claire strode in that direction.

"Where are you going?"

"To answer it."

"Wait." Elizabeth protectively stepped in front of her. "Better let me." She was fairly sure ghosts didn't ring doorbells. But it certainly couldn't be a neighbor bringing cookies.

Nathan Thorpe stood on the stoop of the cozy house, holding a brimming plate wrapped in tinfoil. Walnut-chocolate chip. His specialty. He'd heard the new people had moved in and wanted to welcome them to town. Blayton didn't get many visitors. Full-fledged transplants were even rarer. Nathan couldn't recall the last time a new family had moved here. Might have been the Wilcutts when they bought the old mill store and converted it to a pool hall/saloon.

The door opened just a crack, and Nathan noticed the chain had been latched. A pretty face peered out at him. From his limited point of view, she appeared to be in her thirties and have captivating dark eyes. At least one of them.

"Can I help you?" she asked in a big-city voice that sounded very sophisticated. She also seemed a little skittish, like she wasn't used to living outside of suburbia. Could be the solitude was getting to her. But if that was the case after just one day, this poor lady was in for a long haul.

He smiled warmly. "Just thought I'd stop by and welcome you to Blayton."

She surveyed his khaki-colored uniform along with the gun in his holster. "You're the sheriff?"

He extended his plate. "Nathan Thorpe. Nice to meet you."

"Since when do cops bring cookies?" a girl asked over the woman's shoulder.

She turned and whispered back to a shorter person Nathan took to be her daughter. "I don't know."

Now there were two dark eyes in the door crack, one of them belonging to a face that was younger. Boy, city folk were weird. He'd nearly forgotten that part.

"Uh," Nathan began uncertainly, hedging his way back toward the stairs. "I can just leave these on the steps."

"Wait! Don't go." The door slammed shut, and he heard the chain slide off. A split second later, it opened again, and a stunning brunette greeted him. She was petite and wore jeans and a long-sleeved T-shirt. The teenage daughter beside her was dressed in a similar way, but her jeans were torn. Nathan gathered this was the fashion, and not that the girl had fallen and scraped her knees. He'd seen other kids dress like this as well. Thrift-store chic, his niece called it. "I'm so sorry. I... We...didn't mean to be rude. It's just that we weren't expecting anybody."

"Perfectly fine. I understand." He reached in his wallet and flipped open his credentials. "If it makes you feel any better, this proves I'm the real McCoy." He handed them over, still holding the cookie plate in his left hand.

"I can take that," the girl offered helpfully. Though he surmised it was because she'd caught a whiff of chocolate chips. Nathan's cookies had taken first prize at the county fair for three years running. Not that he ever bragged on himself. Other people did it for him.

Nathan passed her the cookies as the mom flipped shut his credentials and returned them. "I apologize for giving you a hard time." She had a youthful face, but those tell-tale crinkles around her eyes said she'd spent a lot of time worrying. Nathan knew it must be hard raising a girl on her own. The high school secretary said there hadn't even been a father's name listed on the matriculation form. He set his jaw in sympathy for this family, knowing that deadbeat dads weren't just a big-city ailment. Sadly, they were commonplace everywhere.

"I don't blame you for being cautious," he said kindly. "In fact, caution's often a good thing."

"Especially at three-way stops," the girl cut in.

"Exactly." His eyes twinkled and Elizabeth couldn't help but notice their shade, a heady mixture of blue and brown with just a hint of green around the irises. An unusual blend of color complemented by his uniform and tawny brown hair. He appeared to be about her age and was incredibly handsome, solid across the chest with a lean, athletic build. He tipped his hat toward Claire. "Nice to see we've got another good driver in town. I've got my hands full with the bad ones."

"Oh no, I don't—"

"She doesn't drive yet," Elizabeth rushed in, her words overlapping with Claire's. She smiled sweetly at her daughter. "But the time's coming soon."

"I'm sure she'll do fine." He shot each a cordial smile.

"I'm sorry," the woman said politely. "I'm Elizabeth Jennings. And this is my daughter, Claire."

"Pleasure," he said with a nod. "I didn't mean to keep you. Just wanted to let you know that I'm here, if you ever need anything."

Elizabeth's gaze inadvertently traveled to his left hand. At least, she thought her gaze was inadvertent. Surely she wasn't checking for a ring. Although she couldn't help but notice, there wasn't one. Not even a tan line left from where one might have been.

"How will we reach you?" Elizabeth asked.

He shot her a grin and her old-enough-to-know-better heart fluttered.

"Dial 9-1-1."

"Isn't that for emergencies?"

His brow rose in a pleased expression. "Will you be calling me otherwise?"

Elizabeth's cheeks flamed. "I meant, just in case it's something minor. A question, maybe."

He cocked his chin to the side. "9-1-1 will do. We don't get many true emergencies. Martha won't mind."

"Martha?"

"She mans the phones and for the most part spends her days extremely bored. I'm sure she'd welcome the chance to chat with you."

Elizabeth eyed him uncertainly. "Well, all right, if you're sure."

"Wouldn't be opposed myself," he muttered, turning away.

Elizabeth leaned out the door. "What's that?"

His neck colored slightly as he set his eyes on hers. "I said, call any time. No question is too big or too small."

"Ask him, Mom," her daughter urged.

"Do you know anything about the house next door?"

"The old Fenton place?" he asked, intrigued. "I know everything about it. Why?"

"We thought we saw someone in there," Claire said.

"Or something," Elizabeth added quickly. "Of course, it could have been just some shadows."

"What about the light?" Claire prodded with obvious concern.

"Light?"

"There was a sliver of something," Elizabeth said. "I don't know. It was too early for moonlight. I saw it too."

"Hmm." Nathan reached up and stroked his chin. "Could it have looked like this...?" He unhitched the flashlight from his belt and clicked it on, spreading broad beams across the stoop's floorboards.

Elizabeth swallowed hard. "You mean someone was in there? A person?"

Nathan appeared mildly amused. "Most certainly." He clicked off the flashlight, then clipped it back to his belt. "That was me."

"You?" Elizabeth and Claire asked in unison.

"Bob Robeson, the realtor, gave me a key. I stop by to check in once in a while. Ensure nothing is amiss."

Elizabeth felt her stomach churn. "Amiss how?"

"Nothing to trouble over," he answered. "Kid stuff. This time of year, especially. Sometimes teens play pranks. Dare each other to sneak inside and then spend the night. Nobody's ever made it, as far as I can tell."

"Is the place haunted?" Claire asked in all seriousness.

Nathan perused her kindly. "The house is old, sure. With a couple of strange legends attached. But haunted? Not likely."

Elizabeth was about to ask about those strange legends but stopped herself. Claire seemed on edge enough as it was. No need to go upsetting her child further with some idle, small-town lore. Besides, if Nathan assured them nothing was wrong, then what did the two of them have to worry about? He seemed an upright enough individual and was a man of the law besides.

"We appreciate you stopping by," she told him.

"And thanks for the cookies," Claire added.

"No problem, ladies. Enjoy the rest of your evening."

Then he walked down the path and cut across the neighbor's yard, heading to the drive around back.

"Where's his cruiser?" Claire asked.

"He probably parked it behind the house." She shut the door and locked it up tight, turning the dead bolt and sliding the chain in place for extra security.

"That was nice of him to bring cookies," Claire said.

"Yes," Elizabeth agreed. "Why don't we have a few with two cold glasses of milk?"

Later that night, Elizabeth walked to the window to draw the blinds as she prepared for bed. Across the country road abutting her house sat the empty graveyard. Moonlight glinted off tombstones as a hoot owl called. The window was up just a tad to let in the breeze and freshen the air. Though this house couldn't be more than five years old, it smelled as musty and stale as an old cupboard. A floorboard creaked, and

Elizabeth's heart pounded. Her gaze traveled to the side window facing the neighboring house. The rockers next door swayed gently in soft gusts of wind. Now who's letting her imagination get the best of her?

Elizabeth tugged shut the window, thinking she'd never sleep a wink hearing things go creak in the night. Suddenly, something caught her eye, and her blood ran cold. There, straight in her line of vision and at the highest point on the hill, sat two newly dug graves. It seemed impossible that she could have missed them before, mounds of fresh earth heaped high upon each, but she couldn't recall having seen them at all. Elizabeth scolded herself for being spooked by what was obviously a routine occurrence. Of course people were buried there. She just hadn't expected to take a daily head count.

Thank goodness their stay here was only temporary and that she wouldn't need to worry over their imperfect dwelling for too long. As soon as she was able, she'd investigate alternate lodging. In the meantime, she had other priorities. Claire started school on Monday, and Elizabeth had serious work to do. She had the key to the old newspaper shop and planned to make the place gleam like new.

Chapter Two

The next morning, Elizabeth surveyed the rundown corner shop that was to become her new work home. A worn wooden sign beside the weathered door read The Town Gazette in stenciled lettering. The front window was clouded over with cobwebs gathering on the inside. Through its murky pane, she spied an old wooden desk, swivel chair, and what appeared to be an ancient manual typewriter draped in a leather cover. Elizabeth wondered how long this paper had been out of commission. She thought her boss in Richmond said ten years. From the looks of this place, nothing had been happening in the Blayton periodical business for over a half century. She stared down at the key in her hand thinking she might as well let herself in and get busy straightening up. She just prayed it had modern conveniences like electricity and indoor plumbing. Wireless service would be nice too, but was probably too much to hope for. She'd need to call somebody local to have that installed.

"This place sure has seen better days."

Elizabeth peered over her shoulder to find Nathan standing there, sunlight bouncing off his hat. She couldn't help but notice it had warmed up quite a bit these past few days. It was only nine o'clock, and already she felt overheated in her sweater. "Nathan," she said with surprise. "It's great to see you."

"You too." He smiled. "Need any help opening up?"

"I'm assuming the key will turn in the lock."

He glanced past her and stared through the window. "I suppose I should have asked if you need help picking up. Not exactly tidy in there."

"I think it's mostly dust and cobwebs." She slid the key in the lock and jimmied it open to demonstrate. But when she pushed open the door, Elizabeth fell back with a gasp. "Oh," she said, choking on the word "Worse than I thought." Stale air hung heavy as dust assaulted her lungs.

Nathan followed her into the shop, covering his mouth with his sleeve. "I think we should open some windows." He pointed past the desk and typewriter. "There are a few more in back."

She nodded, and he strode across the room, heaving a couple of sashes skyward and sending a blast of autumn breezes into the room. "Keep the front door propped awhile," he told her. "That will help some of this clear out while we get to work."

"We?" Elizabeth asked in surprise.

"I can't let you handle this alone." He gave her a serious frown, but his hazel eyes twinkled. "Could get dangerous."

"Dangerous?"

"You could be attacked by dust bunnies."

Elizabeth burst out laughing. "That's really nice of you, but don't you have a beat to walk or something?"

"I'm on it." He patted the radio strapped to his belt. "Anything comes up, the dispatcher can reach me here."

Elizabeth didn't see how she could inconvenience him to help her on a cleaning mission. Then again, there were some awfully big newspaper bins in the corner she wasn't sure she could move by herself. "I'll tell you what," she said. "I'll let you help with the heavy lifting, but I'll do the cleaning. This is my"—she glanced around the room with a grimace—"place of business after all."

"It will be a great place," he assured her, "once it's all neatened up. And, it's got the best view in town."

"Oh?" Elizabeth followed his gaze out the dirty window and across the street to a quaint little coffee shop. Nestled right beside it hung a placard proudly stating Town Sheriff.

"Your office is right over there?"

"Yes, ma'am," he said, never taking his eyes off hers.

"Then I guess I'll always feel safe when I'm working."

"That's the general idea," he answered. "Helping the folks in Blayton feel safe."

But even as he said it, Elizabeth felt dangerously close to losing her way. For the past twelve years since Claire's dad had left, she'd resolutely steeled her heart against going astray. She had two important jobs to focus on. First, she needed to tend to Claire and provide stability, serving as both mother and father in the absence of a second parent. Next, she had to ensure there was always food on the table and a roof over their heads, because, if she failed at that, it wouldn't matter what kind of great mom she was. Without supplying life's basic needs, she'd be letting her daughter down. From time to time, Elizabeth had noticed an attractive man. She'd even spoken with a few and had gone out more than once for a cup of coffee. But the moment she'd been asked on a nighttime date, her heart backed down. She couldn't drag herself, much less her tender child, through another potentially traumatizing relationship. The stakes were simply too high.

"I'm sure you do a great job."

"I do what I can. Plus," he added, "I've got a good deputy to help me."

"I don't believe I've met the deputy."

"No, I suppose you haven't." He studied her thoughtfully. "In fact, I'll bet you've met almost nobody in town."

Elizabeth shook her head. "Apart from the school secretary and you." She glanced down at the bucket of cleaning supplies she'd toted in. "And, oh yeah, the nice lady at the Dollar Store where I bought all these. I believe she said her name was Jane?"

"Janet Campbell. Nice gal. Married to my deputy in fact."

He smiled warmly, and Elizabeth's breath caught in her throat. This time, she didn't believe it was from the dusty air. It was in the way he looked at her, and each time he did, he seemed to be looking deeper. Way down into her soul to the secret part of her that screamed, *I haven't had a boyfriend in forever and have almost forgotten how to converse with a very hot, single man!* "Really?" She was embarrassed to hear her voice come out as a squeak.

"Almost everyone in Blayton's connected somehow. You stay here long enough," he said with a wink, "you'll become connected to someone too."

It was impossible to tell if he was flirting or just being friendly. She'd been out of practice longer than she knew. "I'm hoping that Claire and I will make some friends."

"You've already got one." He adjusted his hat. "How did you like the cookies?"

Elizabeth's face warmed all over. "Oh gosh, I didn't thank you! I'm so sorry." She swallowed hard to stop herself from stammering like an idiot as he just stared down at her with an appraising smile. "They were delicious. Thanks. World's best chocolate chip. Not a one is left."

"It's good to know they were appreciated."

Elizabeth admitted to herself she'd appreciated more than the cookies. She'd been happy Nathan had stopped by and felt glad to have the chance to get to know him. With him headquartered right across the street, it might prove easy to get to know him better. Her foolish heart leapt at the possibility he might feel the same. "You don't really need to stay here and help... I'm sure you've got things to do."

"A few," he said with a grin. "But I don't mind moving some boxes first."

After he'd hauled some dusty old crates out back and shifted the furniture into position at Elizabeth's direction, Nathan folded his arms with a nod. "I think that just about does it." While he'd been working, she'd been busily dusting the room and mopping the old hardwood floors with oil soap. In no time at all, the place had been transformed from dreary into a space with actual potential. All she had left to do was clean the windows and go through the desk and filing cabinet drawers.

"It looks a thousand times better already," she proclaimed, leaning into her mop. "I've got to be honest. It was a little scary at first."

Nathan viewed her with understanding. "A lot of things seem scarier than they are. It appeared awful. Until you got to know it—one cobweb at a time."

Elizabeth laughed, enjoying his sense of humor. "I wish I could do something to repay you."

He replaced the hat he'd removed while he'd been working, and tipped it toward her. "All in a day's work."

"Will you come to dinner sometime?" she asked, blurting out the words the moment the thought had occurred and before its ramifications could form in her brain. A simple invitation to a meal didn't have to mean she was hitting on him. Did it?

She watched his neck deepen a shade behind the high rim of his collar, thinking maybe it did. "I'd like that," he answered. "Be very pleased to have dinner with you and Claire.

"But first," he said. "I think I should introduce you around. Help you get to know the town's folk a bit."

"That would be nice."

"How about you stop by the station when you finish up here? If you're not too tuckered out from cleaning, that is."

Elizabeth didn't believe her being overtired later seemed likely. Not when just looking in his eyes left her feeling energized. Almost like a teen girl on the verge of a... Oh no, not that... Elizabeth's heart skipped a beat. A crush.

Nathan headed back across the street to his office in a happy mood. Of all the strangers who'd come to

Blayton since he'd been here, Elizabeth was by far the most interesting. Didn't hurt that she was very pretty besides. Her daughter seemed like a nice girl too. And nice teenagers were a bonus in this town. He thought of his niece, Melody, wishing she'd get her meanness under control. He knew it had to do with things at home. Nathan's sister, Belle, was a single mom doing her best with the girl. But her job at the library kept her busy afternoons and weekends, too. Melody was bitter over all the things she had to miss out on due to her mom's work schedule, and their tight family finances. She hadn't been able to participate in cheerleading or go on the class field trip. Nathan helped them out when he could, but the fact was he didn't make a ton of money. Then again, Nathan wasn't in his job for the money. He had bigger reasons for being the sheriff, most of them centered on setting things right. Everyone here had something they wanted, a goal they were working toward it seemed. At times they were aware of it, and at others they weren't. Like in Melody's case, where her duty was to grow into the caring young woman her family knew she had the ability to be.

Nathan made his way into the station and spotted Martha at the front desk, her nose in a book. The middle-aged woman with red hair and a round face glanced up with a pleasant smile. Her real job was manning the 9-1-1 line, but since it seldom rang, he never commented on her rabid reading habit. "Morning, Sherriff," she said, setting a bookmark in her book. Nathan noticed there was a stack of others by her coffee mug, several of which he'd offer to return to the library when he visited Belle later. "Can I get you some coffee?"

"Thanks, Martha, but I'm set for now."

And he was too. Just the thought that he'd be seeing Elizabeth later put an extra skip in his step and made him feel charged all over like he'd already had loads of caffeine.

"Morning, Nathan!" Bernie called from the back office. His deputy sat with his feet propped on his desk, working the morning crossword puzzle—from a decade ago. Since the Gazette had gone out of business, Bernie didn't have a regular paper to feed his addiction. So Belle had been kind enough to dig up a heap of out-of-print editions from the archive room at the library. She didn't mind getting rid of them, as they'd already been scanned and saved in electronic format and were headed to recycle anyway.

For Bernie's part, he was pleased as punch that he could engage in his favorite pastime and cheat when the need arose. More than once Nathan had caught Bernie sneaking a peek at the following week's paper to nab a word or two that had vexed him from the solution box. Though Bernie was barely pushing thirty, he often came out with real old-timey expressions that made him sound like he was more than twice that age. Nathan wasn't sure why, though he suspected it had to do with the number of years he'd spent in Blayton.

The pace of things was slower here, and everything a little retro. But still, when Nathan had arrived, the town felt right. It was a warm and welcoming town, and Nathan liked the people. Everyone was genuine, and genuinely concerned about each other. Except for a few outliers that were still coming along. Nathan sat at his desk, thinking of his niece, Melody. Eventually, she'd make progress too. Because as backward as Blayton seemed, folks here always tended to move forward—sooner or later.

Claire was just shutting her locker when two girls accosted her, one on either side. The first one was skinny and blonde with a boyish figure and cool blue eyes. "You're new here, aren't you?" she asked in a tone that wasn't quite friendly.

Claire glanced warily at the second girl, a shorter redhead, who stood nearby clutching her algebra book to her chest. "Today's my first day."

"That's what we thought," the smaller girl said. "My name's Joy."

"Yeah, yeah. And I'm Melody, but that's really beside the point."

Claire steadied herself on her heels, not sure what to expect. A warm welcome to Blayton High didn't appear in the offering. "What is the point?" she asked as evenly as she could.

Melody gave an exaggerated sigh. "You moved next to the Fenton place, didn't you?"

"I'm not sure I—"

"The creepy old house?" Joy filled in.

Mirth danced in Melody's eyes as she leaned forward. Claire instinctively wanted to inch back but held her ground. "You did hear it was haunted?"

"I don't believe in ghosts."

Melody and Joy exchanged glances, and a shiver raced down Claire's spine as if she'd been exposed to a chill.

"Then you're in for some fun," Melody said.

"Ghostly fun," Joy agreed.

"Thanks for the tip, but I was on my way to lunch."

Claire tried to step past them, but Melody blocked her path with her tall frame. "The lady who lived there was murdered, you know. In her sleep."

Joy solemnly nodded. "Nobody found her for weeks."

"Weeks and weeks." Melody lowered her voice in a vicious whisper. "And when they did… Her old tabby cat was eating up the corpse."

Joy assented with light brown eyes. "Poor thing was starving."

Claire's stomach clenched. Not so much at their ridiculous story as at the thought two ninth graders could be so cruel, purposely tormenting a newcomer. Not that she hadn't seen the same thing happen in her hometown. But there, it always happened to someone else. Claire was never on the receiving end. Nor on the side dishing it out. Claire simply didn't have it in her.

"What are you two up to now?" someone asked, approaching. Claire peered over Joy's shoulder to see a cute boy with dark brown hair and eyes moseying down the hall.

Melody turned with delight. "Perry! I didn't think you were here today?"

"Got in late," he answered, still walking forward. He gave Claire a lazy smile, the sort that turned up higher in one corner, and her heart did a tiny cartwheel. "Hello? And you are…?"

"I'm Claire," she said, relieved at last to see a friendly face.

"Nice to meet you, Claire. I'm sure Melody and Joy have been showing you the ropes?"

More like trying to trip me with them, Claire thought but didn't say. Instead, she answered, "We were just getting acquainted."

Melody narrowed her gaze at Claire in warning. As evil as she and her sidekick, Joy, were, Melody apparently didn't want Perry finding out. "We were just telling her how great it is having a new girl in our class," Melody lied.

When Perry glanced at Joy for confirmation, she added, "And welcoming her to the school."

Perry seemed to be weighing whether or not to believe this. "Well, now that your welcome is done, you probably have some place to be."

"Oh no, I don't think I—" Melody began.

"Don't you both have lunch detention?"

Joy's face grew long. "He's right, Mel. Maybe we'd better get going. Mr. Harris will tack on another day if we're late."

Perry shrugged at them like, what can you do?

Melody's face flushed pink.

"Catch you later," Perry said.

Both girls pursed their lips, hesitating. It was obvious they were reluctant to leave, especially Melody, who had barely taken her eyes off Perry since he'd gotten here.

He made an exaggerated display of pulling his cell from his pocket to check the time.

"Yeah, right," Melody finally said. "We'd better go."

"See ya," Joy added, addressing Perry before scooting off.

Perry's gaze trailed the pair as they traveled down the hall. "Hope they didn't give you trouble."

"Trouble?" Claire asked, feeling her own face flame.

His eyes fell on hers. "They're not the nicest duo at Blayton, if you know what I'm saying."

And boy, hadn't Claire experienced that firsthand. Still, she said, "Nothing I can't handle."

"You look like you can probably handle a lot."

"Hey!"

His lips crept up in a grin. "I meant that as a compliment."

Claire shifted on her feet, feeling her tensions ease. "Thanks."

Perry motioned to the brown bag she gripped in her hand. "What's for lunch?"

"Peanut butter and jelly."

"Can't go wrong with that."

"Nope."

"You got someone to eat with?"

Claire lowered her chin. "Not exactly."

"You do now," he said when she looked up. "I know a great spot in the sun. No one will bother us there."

"You mean it's far from lunch detention?"

Perry laughed. "Way far. Clear around the corner and on the other side of the building."

"Sounds very cool."

Perry led Claire around the big brick building to a back patio dotted with picnic tables. A few facing the football field were empty. He motioned for her to sit, and she slid onto a bench while he sat across from her. "So, how come you're in Blayton?" he asked, extracting a submarine sandwich from his bag and unwrapping it. It was loaded to the brim with all sorts of meats and cheeses, heaped with lettuce and tomatoes too. Claire stared down at her own sandwich, slightly envious. Of course, she had nobody to blame but herself. She'd insisted long ago that her mom give up on preparing her lunch. She was too old for that and could certainly slap some peanut butter and jelly on wheat bread herself. She took a bite, thinking it wasn't half bad, though not nearly as delicious as Perry's sub appeared.

"It was my mom's idea. Not her idea, really. Her boss's. To tell you the truth," Claire continued, "I don't think she wanted to come here any more than I did."

Perry stopped eating to look at her. "Blayton's not so bad, once you get used to it."

She studied his warm brown eyes. "How long have you been here?"

He appeared thoughtful a moment. "About three years."

"So you went to middle school at Kenan?"

He swigged from his water bottle. "And man, wasn't that wild."

"What do you mean?"

"Just that it was middle school, you know?"

She smiled like she did, but wasn't sure what he meant.

"Crazy kids doing crazy stuff." He shook his head. "And Melody and Joy? Believe it or not, they were arch enemies then."

"Really?" She leaned forward with interest. "What happened?"

"Melody started some kind of rumor about Joy that turned the rest of their girlfriends against her. By now, though, most of them have moved on."

"Moved away, you mean?"

"Yeah. That's how it is here. People come and go. More than you'd think for a small town."

Claire polished off the rest of her sandwich and started her apple, considering this. "Where did they go to? Those other girls?"

Perry shrugged. "Who knows? It's not like anybody ever tells us kids. Some mornings you just wake up and people are gone."

An unsettling tingle raced down Claire's spine. She dismissed it as a weird feeling she didn't understand. "I guess families move sometimes. Mine did."

He began chomping on some kettle chips. "Anyway, the point is, after that, neither Melody or Joy had too many friends left, so they decided to stick together. For better or worse."

"Seems like for worse to me."

"You nailed that one." Perry chuckled. "But don't let them get to you, all right? Joy's not so bad. And believe it or not, Melody has her good side."

"If you say so."

"Oh, it's there, I've seen it. She just doesn't like letting people know."

"Why not?"

"It's a power thing. She doesn't want to lose control."

"Of...?"

"Her standing in the school as most popular girl, reigning queen...and closet class bully."

"Wow."

"Yeah, but mostly I think she's afraid of herself."

To Claire's amazement, he opened some tinfoil, exposing a mouthwatering chocolate-chunk brownie. "I'm sorry if this is personal, but I've got to ask."

He met her eyes, and Claire heart rose in her throat. Perry was the cutest boy she'd ever seen. He was certainly the hottest guy she'd ever sat this close to.

"Ye-es?" he prodded with a grin.

Claire felt the perspiration build at her brow. "Who makes your lunch?"

"I do."

"You?"

"Well, okay, I'll be fair. My uncle made the brownies."

"You're pretty lucky to have an uncle like that."

"Don't I know it." He split the brownie in two. "Here," he said, handing her half. "I'll share."

Chapter Three

After eating her packed lunch, Elizabeth finished cleaning out the desk's drawers. Most of the paperwork was decades old, the majority of which could be discarded. She set aside anything that seemed important to ask Nathan about later. If he didn't know, maybe the town librarian would have an inkling regarding whether any of these old news notes held value. Elizabeth sighed and shut the last drawer, eyeing the covered typewriter on the desk. She'd saved its unveiling until the very end. Not knowing what she would find or the condition it might be in, she didn't want to ruin her hopeful anticipation.

Elizabeth was long past employing typewriters, and the only one she'd ever used had been electric. But still, the moment she lifted the worn leather cover, she knew she had a real gem in store. There it sat, the most perfect Royal Quiet DeLuxe, in pristine condition, keys gleaming like they'd been polished yesterday. It was a beauty, shiny, and black with stenciled gold lettering. She took a tentative strike at a key, and it clunked heavily against the cartridge, hitting with forceful precision. Elizabeth instinctively massaged her knuckle, thinking her fingers were nowhere near primed to take that sort of daily beating. Folks back then must have gotten used to it. Then again, they hadn't known any different. Laptop computers with easy-touch keypads were light years away when this was invented. She ran her hand across the top of the machine, thinking it would make a lovely office mascot. She might even position it with some other historic items, like original copies of the Gazette, in the front window. But that could wait until tomorrow. Today, she wanted to be home in time to meet Claire's bus. While she wouldn't precisely be standing on the corner—which would embarrass Claire no end—she did want to be there, perhaps with a fresh batch of goodies in the oven. Elizabeth knew this move was hard on Claire and understood the transition couldn't be easy. She wanted to do everything she could to help smooth things over. But first, she thought, checking the time with a smile, she had a date to keep.

Martha set down her book and stared at Nathan. "You expecting someone, Sheriff?"

"Not really," he said, pacing back toward his office.

Martha glanced down at the carpet and the invisible path he had worn. "Could have fooled me."

Nathan lifted the coffeepot and nonchalantly poured himself a cup. "What would drive you to say that?"

"Oh…just the fact that you've walked back and forth to the front window at least half a dozen times," she said in a lilting tone. "In the past ten minutes! Say, weren't you across the street earlier? Helping that newcomer out?"

Nathan took a sip of java, avoiding her gaze. "I was just being neighborly."

She got that smug little pout on her lips like she did when she thought she knew something. "You made her chocolate chip cookies, didn't you?"

"I make everyone cookies. Everyone new in town, that is."

"Not everyone, Nathan, and you know it."

He set his cup on the edge of her desk. "I do so. When the Wilcutts moved in, I took some to them."

"As I recall, that was lemon bars."

"And the Daniels family—"

"Strudel."

"State what you've got to say, Martha."

She met his gaze with an impish grin. "Just that your chocolate chip cookies spell L-O-V-E."

He squared his chin. "Come on."

"Took first place at the fair, didn't they? As I recall, the blue ribbon read Most Likely Baked Goods by a Bachelor to Make a Woman Fall in—"

"Hello?" The front door pushed open with a whoosh of air and its dangling bell chimed. Nathan's face fired hot as Elizabeth stared at him wide-eyed. "Oh good! It's you."

"Uh-huh," Martha clucked, shooting Nathan a glance.

"Elizabeth! Great." He cleared his throat, which had suddenly constricted. "You done cleaning up over there?"

She nodded, smiling at Martha. "I'm Elizabeth Jennings. We're new in town."

"So I've heard," Martha said, beaming. "Martha Holt." She extended her hand to shake Elizabeth's. "Nice to meet you."

"Same," Elizabeth said. She surveyed the small station with its old-timey radio on display. "Quaint. I've got something of that vintage over at my place."

"The typewriter?" Martha queried.

"That's the one. But how did you—?"

"Used to work with Pinkney Gale. He was the old news editor before you came. Naturally, that was some time ago."

"She probably guessed that from the cobwebs," Nathan added, settling his hat on his head. He turned to Elizabeth with a smile. "Ready to see the town?"

"As long as I'm home by four."

"That's when the high school gets out," Martha explained to Nathan, as if he didn't know. "My girl goes there too," she told Elizabeth.

"Really? That's great. Maybe she and Claire will be friends."

"Better chance of that than of Nathan's niece stepping in."

"Martha, please."

Elizabeth turned to Nathan as he led her toward the door. "Your niece?"

"It's a long story, but she's coming along."

"You kids coming back here after the tour?" Martha shouted after them.

Nathan pulled shut the door with a wink. "Don't count on it."

Once on the street, Elizabeth burst out laughing. "Oh my, that Martha's something! I mean, very nice, but—"

"Yeah," Nathan said. "She knows pretty much everything about everybody. So be careful what you tell her."

Elizabeth laughed again, liking it here. She'd never lived in a small town before. While it clearly was different from the larger metropolis she was used to, it held its own charm. As they turned toward town, Nathan halted suddenly. "Hang on. Would you mind waiting here a second? I forgot something."

"No problem," she said as he bolted back up the front steps to the station. He slipped through the door, then reappeared a moment later holding a stack of books.

"What are those?"

"Promised Martha I'd drop these by the library. We're stopping by there anyway."

Elizabeth eyed him with admiration, thinking that Nathan was the sort of guy who did nice things for everybody, even those who obviously razzed him. She didn't know what Martha had been teasing him about before she'd walked into the station, but Elizabeth had a heady intuition that it had a lot to do with her. Her and the fact that Nathan had offered to show her around. While it was a generous thing to do, Elizabeth suspected it wasn't a welcoming service Nathan provided to everybody. "It's nice of you to introduce me to people."

"I'm happy to do it."

"You really are some kind of sheriff."

He glanced at her, and his hazel eyes twinkled. "Am I?"

"A good kind, I mean."

"A bad kind wouldn't do."

"No."

"Elizabeth," he said, his gaze still on hers, "I'm awfully glad you moved to Blayton."

"Thanks. It's good to be here." And when she said it, the words rang true. Though she'd initially rejected the move and especially had protested it because of her daughter, something deep inside told Elizabeth this was where she and Claire were meant to be.

The next hour sped by in a blur of happy chatter and welcoming faces. They stopped by the Dollar Store and the corner market and met Bernie by the Dairy Queen, where he was filling the tank of his cruiser. But their first stop had been at the library, where Elizabeth met Nathan's sister Belle, the librarian, and he dropped off his haul of books. By the time they walked back to the newspaper shop where Elizabeth had parked, her feet ached and her tongue was all worn out from talking. She hadn't known they could cover so many miles in such a small area, or that she—normally an introvert—would find herself so suddenly extroverted among a passel of strangers. Something was different about Blayton. Elizabeth felt at ease and alive here. It was almost as if the whole rest of her life had been a dream, and she was just now—at age thirty-three—finally waking up.

She and Nathan stood on the sidewalk beside her SUV. "Thanks for taking me around today," she said. "That was special. Really made me feel...included."

"I'm glad." His smile warmed her through and through. "I hope you'll like it here."

She already did. Perhaps a tad too much. Her heart was already beating faster just because he was near. She opened the driver's door, and Nathan tilted his hat.

"Don't think I've forgotten."

"Forgotten?"

"About that dinner invitation."

Elizabeth's pulse pounded in her ears. "Yeah, right," she said, feeling her world flash hot, then cold, then warm again... "I'll call you."

"Just dial 9-1-1," he said with a grin.

When Claire walked in the door, Elizabeth was pulling warm banana bread from the oven. "So, how was school?"

"Okay."

"Just okay? Did you meet anyone?"

"A couple of kids." Claire set her backpack on a chair, then dropped down into another. "Smells good. What's cooking?"

"Banana bread. With pecans, just the way you like it."

Claire seemed mildly distracted. She pulled out her cell and began busily checking for messages. "The service here stinks."

"Cell service?"

"Yeah."

"I'm sorry, hon. These are probably old towers."

"I don't think they even have towers in this place."

Elizabeth turned the hot loaf onto a cooling rack. "Maybe not."

"Even at school, I got only one bar."

"You're not supposed to be using your phone at school."

"I was checking for messages from you," Claire said smoothly.

"Hmm, yes. Well, luckily I didn't call. I'll remember to phone through the office if I ever need to get in touch for some emergency."

Claire's gaze flitted to the landline. "When's the Wi-Fi going in?"

"Sometime this week, I hope."

"I was worried we'd have to do dial-up."

Elizabeth sputtered a laugh. "I don't think Blayton is that retro. Want a piece?" she asked, cutting a steaming slice.

"Sure, thanks." Claire rose to her feet. "I'll get the milk."

"So," Claire asked when they were both settled at the table. "How was your day in town?"

"Fine."

"Fine?"

"Yeah. I mean, great. Things went really well."

"Meet anyone?"

"Lots of folks! Nathan was nice enough to show me around."

Claire raised an eyebrow. "Sheriff Nathan?"

Elizabeth felt unnervingly as if she were under a microscope and that Claire could see right through her. At least straight down to her rapidly pounding heart. "What?"

Claire took a bite of bread. "I think Nathan likes you."

"What makes you say that?"

"I don't know. He looks at you funny."

"Funny how?"

Claire's lips broadened in a grin. "Like he thinks you're hot."

"I'm much too old to be hot."

"No, you're not."

Elizabeth's face warmed. "Thanks, honey. It's nice of you to think so."

"I'm not the only one…" Claire teased.

Elizabeth slapped her arm. "What makes you such an expert all of a sudden?"

"Life."

"Really?"

"And, maybe I met a boy at school."

"Claire!"

"A cool guy. A friend."

"Of course, that's what I thought." But from the stars in her daughter's eyes, Elizabeth believed Claire was interested in being more than friends with this boy. "What's his name?"

"Perry."

"That's a nice name."

"It's a name, Mom. Just a name."

"Right."

"So is Nathan."

"Argh!" Elizabeth leapt to her feet and hugged her girl. "I love you so much."

"I love you too."

"We're going to get through this, you know. This transition. Together."

"I know," Claire said, hugging her back.

Elizabeth awoke with a jolt to a wailing sound. What was that awful cry that sounded like a tortured soul in the night? She clutched the covers to her chest and blinked hard, trying to make out her hazy surroundings. The room came into focus, a haunting glow from a full moon streaking through the window. She'd been so whipped from her day, Elizabeth had forgotten to draw the blinds. She'd slipped into her pajamas in the bathroom, brushed her teeth, and hit the hay like an exhausted farmhand after a tough day. It couldn't have taken her more than five minutes to fall asleep, and her slumber had been deep. Miles deep, until this murky awakening… Something screeched again, its sound ravaging the darkness. Her bedroom door flew open, and Claire raced inside.

"Mom! Did you hear it?" Claire's face was ashen in the moonlight, panic registering in her eyes.

Elizabeth gathered her wits, trying to calm her daughter. "There has to be some logical—"

Reeeoowww! It hollered again, and Claire leapt onto her bed. "What is it?" Claire beseeched as Elizabeth wrapped her in her arms.

"I don't—"

There was the sound of glass breaking and a strange commotion in the house next door. Elizabeth and Claire tentatively rose from the bed, holding hands.

"It came from over there," Claire said, staring out the window. The ancient Victorian stood silent in haunting shadows. Claire squeezed her hand tight. Time was a vacuum as they watched and waited, hearing nothing more as the minutes stretched on.

"I'm calling Nathan," Elizabeth finally said.

"Good idea," Claire replied without loosening her grip.

Twenty minutes later, Nathan returned to their door with a flashlight. "I think I've found your ghost," he said, holding a large tabby cat in one arm.

"What?" Elizabeth asked in shock. For the ten minutes he'd been in there, she'd been a knot of nerves, not knowing what he might find. Not knowing if he'd get hurt. Fearing he might not return at all.

"You poor baby." Claire extended her arms toward the kitty, and Nathan passed him over. "Were you in there all alone?"

"He apparently got into some trouble," Nathan said. "Knocked a mirror off a dresser and broke it clear to pieces."

"That's bad luck," Elizabeth responded.

"Cats have nine lives," Nathan returned with a wry smile.

Elizabeth pondered the cat, now purring loudly in Claire's arms as she scratched him under the chin. "I don't understand. How did he get in there?"

"There's an old basement window that keeps coming loose. Critters crawl in from time to time."

"Some girls at school said old Mrs. Fenton had a cat."

"Don't let those urban legends scare you," Nathan said. "Nothing but nonsense."

"What urban legends?" Elizabeth wanted to know.

"I'll tell you later." Claire lifted the cat toward her chin, nuzzling him closer. "Can we keep him?"

She glanced at Nathan. "He's probably got a home."

"Might at that," Nathan said. "I'll ask around."

"In the meantime?" Claire pleaded.

The cat purred louder as if granting his assent.

"Only for the night," Elizabeth acquiesced. "Until Nathan checks around."

Claire's cheeks glowed bright pink. "Thanks, Mom!" Then she scurried off with the cat, presumably to pour him a bowl of milk.

"I want to thank you for coming by," Elizabeth said to Nathan when it was just the two of them. "I didn't know what to do. I mean, who else to call."

"You did the right thing," Nathan told her. "In fact, it made Martha's night. It's the second call she's gotten all month!"

"Who was the first one from?"

"Confidential. Police business."

"Of course."

"Though I can likely predict that third call."

"Oh?"

A slow grin spread across his handsome face. "It's coming from 312 Oak Street."

"But this is 312 Oak Street."

"Exactly," Nathan said, pinning her in place with his gaze.

Elizabeth felt her body warm from head to toe. "Why, Sheriff," she flirted, "are you angling to get asked to dinner again?"

"Might be."

"What's your Friday like?"

"I believe I could work in an opening. That is, if you don't mind my being on call."

"I suspect the sheriff is always on call."

"Yes, ma'am."

"Then, it's a date." The moment the words flew from her mouth, Elizabeth kicked herself a billion times. A date? Elizabeth? Really? "An engagement, I mean. An agreement to have supper."

Nathan tipped his hat with a smile. "If that means you're cooking, I accept."

A few nights later, Nathan sat across the kitchen table from his sister, Belle, and her girl, Melody, as they all ate sloppy joes. "Appreciate you having me over."

"We like having you over," Belle said with sincere blue eyes. "Besides..." She rolled her gaze toward her daughter. "You're a good influence around here."

Nathan set down his sandwich, picking up his sister's cue. "You behaving yourself at school?"

The girl's face fell, but she didn't answer.

"Melody got detention again."

Nathan addressed his niece, unable to mask his disappointment. "Oh, hon, really?"

"It wasn't my fault!"

"Don't go blaming Joy," Belle said sternly. "She told the principal that shaving creaming the girls' locker room was your idea."

"Easy for her to say."

Nathan evenly met her gaze. "You've got to stop getting yourself into mischief, Melody Anne. And start acting like a grown lady. You're practically sixteen now."

Melody huffed and dabbed her mouth with her napkin. "Can I be excused now?" she asked her mom.

Belle sternly addressed her child. "Your uncle's talking to you."

"Yeah? What's he gonna do? Throw me in jail?"

"Melody!" Belle tried to stop her daughter as she sprang from the table.

"It's all right," Nathan said softly. "Let her go."

"But I can't let her talk to you like that."

Nathan sadly shook his head, sorry for Belle and the trials Melody put her through. "I'll have a chat with her later."

After he'd helped Belle tidy the kitchen, Nathan rapped at Melody's door.

"Go away!" she yelled through it.

"You're not in trouble, if that's what you're thinking," Nathan called back.

He heard padded footfalls, then Melody's door cracked open. She stared at him with suspicion. "Why not?"

"Because I know you didn't mean to."

"The locker room?"

"Be disrespectful."

Melody heaved a sigh, and suddenly appeared fragile, like the angelic seven-year-old she used to be before her world went sour. "I'm sorry, Uncle Nathan."

"Everything passes, you know?"

"What do you mean?"

"The hard times, Melody Anne." He drew a breath, then released it. "I know it's not easy being fifteen. I was that age once myself. And I know it especially hasn't been easy on you...for a lot of reasons. But that doesn't mean you have to take it out on everyone else."

She hung her head, but he could tell she was listening.

"Your mom loves you a good deal. And listen up, kiddo. Your uncle here loves you too. You've got two great folks in your corner. That's more than a lot of people can say these days, you know."

She raised a hand to wipe her cheek, and Nathan suspected she was crying. "But why did he have to do it? Why?" When she raised her gaze to his, her eyes were bleary. "I begged him not to go, really I did. But he just picked up his suitcase and—"

Nathan pulled her into his arms as she broke down. "There, there," he said, gently patting her back. "I know."

She gripped him tightly, sobbing against his chest and Nathan's heart split in two. He didn't know how

Belle's ex had been heartless enough to do it, but somehow he had. Up and walked out on his perfectly decent wife and child. None of them ever knew why. And nobody knew where he'd gone. Those were the sticking points. "But you listen up, little girl. There is one guy here who's never going to leave you, you hear?"

Tears streamed down her cheeks and her chin trembled. "Swear to God?"

"Cross my heart and hope to die."

Belle walked in, quickly surmising the scene and wrapped her arms around them. "We're family," she told them both, "and family sticks together."

Nathan held them tighter. "Yes, we do."

Later, on the front porch, Belle told him, "I want to thank you for that in there. It really helped. Having you around always helps."

"I'm glad to be here when I can. I just wish I could do more."

"You do plenty." She shared a weary smile. "You doing anything on Friday? They're having Harvest Night at the orchard, and I thought I'd take Melody."

Nathan knew Harvest Night was a good time, complete with hayrides and hot apple cider, but this Friday he had plans. "Love to, but some other time."

Belle curiously eyed her brother. "Got something else going on?"

"I might."

"Something involving that pretty brunette you introduced me to?"

"You women are so suspicious." But when he turned his back, Nathan's lips parted in a grin.

"I want to hear all about it!" Belle called after him.

He strolled off, breaking into a bright whistle.

"I'm serious! Saturday! Over coffee!"

Nathan held up a hand in a wave but kept on walking. Spilling to Belle after his night at Elizabeth's? Like that was going to happen. It wasn't such a big deal anyway. He was just going for dinner with the two of them, Elizabeth and Claire. It wasn't like he had a date. Not that he'd know what to do with one if he had it. Nathan mentally tried to calculate the last time he'd been out with an eligible woman. An eligible woman he felt attracted to, and who hadn't been one of Belle's or Martha's set-ups. But his mind grew foggy and he couldn't think that far back. Especially since all he was eager to do now was look ahead. The day after tomorrow, he'd be sitting down to supper with the Jennings. He didn't know why, but there was an unexpected lift in his heart just at the thought.

** End of Excerpt **

The Ghost Next Door (A Love Story) is available in ebook and paperback at online retailers now. Please visit http://www.ginnybairdromance.com for details.